I should leave now.

Bryce's heart beat faster as his gaze clung to Amy's. She had the most incredible eyes. A man could fall into those eyes and never want to come out.

Afterward, he could never think how it happened. All he knew was he fully intended to say goodbye and the next minute he was kissing her. Not a peck, either. A real kiss. One that made his head swim and every hormone in his body leap to attention.

Holy crow, he thought as he raised his head and they stared at each other. *What have I done?*

And more important...what do I do now?

Dear Reader,

It's October, the time of year when crisper temperatures and waning daylight turns our attention to more indoor pursuits— such as reading! And we at Silhouette Special Edition are happy to supply you with the material. We begin with *Marrying Molly,* the next in bestselling author Christine Rimmer's BRAVO FAMILY TIES series. A small-town mayor who swore she'd break the family tradition of becoming a mother *before* she becomes a wife finds herself nonetheless in the very same predicament. And the father-to-be? The very man who's out to get her job....

THE PARKS EMPIRE series continues with Lois Faye Dyer's *The Prince's Bride,* in which a wedding planner called on to plan the wedding of an exotic prince learns that *she's* the bride-to-be! Next, in *The Devil You Know,* Laurie Paige continues her popular SEVEN DEVILS miniseries with the story of a woman determined to turn her marriage of convenience into the real thing. Patricia Kay begins her miniseries THE HATHAWAYS OF MORGAN CREEK, the story of a Texas baking dynasty (that's right, *baking!*), with *Nanny in Hiding,* in which a young mother on the run from her abusive ex seeks shelter in the home of Bryce Hathaway—and finds so much more. In *Wrong Twin, Right Man* by Laurie Campbell, a man who feels he failed his late wife terribly gets another chance to make it up—to her twin sister. At least he *thinks* she's her twin.... And in Wendy Warren's *Making Babies,* a newly divorced woman whose ex-husband denied her the baby she always wanted, finds a willing candidate—in the guilt-ridden lawyer who represented the creep in his divorce!

Enjoy all six of these reads, and come back again next month to see what's up in Silhouette Special Edition.

Take care,

Gail Chasan
Senior Editor

Please address questions and book requests to:
Silhouette Reader Service
U.S.: 3010 Walden Ave., P.O. Box 1325, Buffalo, NY 14269
Canadian: P.O. Box 609, Fort Erie, Ont. L2A 5X3

Nanny in Hiding

PATRICIA KAY

Silhouette®

SPECIAL EDITION®

Published by Silhouette Books

America's Publisher of Contemporary Romance

This book is dedicated to my granddaughter Kaylee,
who is already showing signs of becoming
a great writer! Love you, sweetheart.

 SILHOUETTE BOOKS

ISBN 0-373-24642-0

NANNY IN HIDING

Copyright © 2004 by Patricia A. Kay

Visit Silhouette Books at www.eHarlequin.com

Printed in U.S.A.

PATRICIA KAY,

formerly writing as Trisha Alexander, is the *USA TODAY* bestselling author of more that thirty contemporary romances. She lives in Houston, Texas. To learn more about her, visit her Web site at www.patriciakay.com.

CAST OF CHARACTERS—
The Hathaways of Morgan Creek

Stella Morgan Hathaway (90 years old)—Matriarch of the Hathaway family.

Jonathan Morgan Hathaway (67 years old)—Stella's only son.

Kathleen Bryce Hathaway (63 years old)—Jonathan's wife.

Bryce Hathaway (40 years old)—A widower, he is Jonathan and Kathleen's only son.

Amy Jordan (32 years old)—On the run from her ex-husband, Amy hides among the Hathaways.

Calista Jordan (3 years old)—Amy's daughter.

Cole Jordan (37 years old)—Amy's ex-husband.

Chloe Hathaway Standish (36 years old)—The oldest Hathaway daughter.

Lorna Morgan Hathaway (32 years old)—The middle Hathaway daughter.

Claudia Elizabeth Hathaway (28 years old)—The youngest Hathaway daughter.

Greg Standish (38 years old)—Chloe's husband.

Cameron Kathleen Standish (14 years old)—Chloe and Greg's daughter.

Stella Ann Hathaway (8 years old)—Bryce's older daughter.

Susan Adele Hathaway (7 years old)—Bryce's younger daughter.

Prologue

"Mommy! Lookit me! I can do a summersot!"

Amy Jordan smiled at her three-year-old's exuberance. "It's summer*sault*, sweetie. Can you say *sault?*"

"Sot," Calista said, grinning up at her mother from her upside-down position.

Amy chuckled. *L*s and *R*s were hard for her daughter to get her tongue around. As Calista continued doing her version of a summersault, Amy glanced at her watch. With a pang, she saw there was only about ten minutes left of her allotted visiting time.

As always, at the thought of leaving Calista, Amy's spirits plummeted. She eyed Mrs. Witherspoon, who sat placidly knitting. What was the woman thinking? Did she have any idea how painful these visits were for Amy? Just how hard it was for her to leave her daughter week in and week out?

The strict rules of visitation Amy was required to follow nearly overwhelmed her with despair. After all the abuse she had suffered, the unfairness of the judge's decree made her want to scream or weep or both. But as hard as it was for her to maintain control and leave Calista, it was even harder on her baby. Remembering the scene last time, Amy girded herself to be strong and make parting as easy for Calista as she could.

To that end, she slowly rose from the floor where she'd been playing with her daughter for the past three hours.

"Almost time?" Mrs. Witherspoon said, putting down her knitting.

Amy swallowed the lump in her throat and nodded.

"Before you go, let me just run to the bathroom."

Amy's heart banged against her chest as she realized what the woman had said. Forcing her voice not to give away her sudden excitement, she said, "Okay."

The moment Mrs. Witherspoon disappeared down the hall, Amy flew into the dining room. Grabbing one of the chairs, she hurried toward the bathroom where she jammed the chair up and under the door-knob. Then she raced back to the living room, snatched up Calista, grabbed her purse and ran out the door.

"Mommy?"

"It's okay, honey." Reaching her car, which was parked in the driveway, Amy unlocked it with shaking hands. Earlier, she'd covered the car seat she was never without and now she pulled the blanket off and somehow managed to get Calista buckled in without losing more than a couple of precious minutes. She had no idea how long she'd have before Mrs. Witherspoon realized what had happened and managed to free herself from the bathroom and alert Cole that Amy had taken off with Calista.

All she knew was this was her chance, the first opportunity she'd had in the year since the divorce, and she wasn't going to blow it. She'd been ready for months. Every time she visited with Calista, the trunk of her car had been packed for a getaway. Everything the two of them needed to begin a new life was in that trunk: clothing, toys and games for Calista, food, money, a first-aid kit, sleeping bags. She even had fake ID, thanks to the underground network that aided abused women and children and helped them escape the men who persecuted them.

By now Amy's heart was beating so fast it scared her, and when her car didn't immediately start, she thought she might pass out. But the engine caught on the next try, and within minutes Amy was doing a sedate thirty miles an hour—she was terrified of getting stopped for speeding—and heading for the highway that would take her away from Mobile.

She still couldn't believe it had happened. Never before, in all the time since the divorce, had Mrs. Witherspoon left her alone with Calista. Amy had begun to believe it might never happen, yet she had never given up hope.

"Mommy?" Calista said from the backseat. "Are we goin' to the store?"

"No, sweetie. We're going on a vacation."

"A 'cation?"

"Uh-huh."

"Is Daddy coming?"

"Nope. Just you and me."

"Okay," Calista said happily.

Amy smiled, even though inside she was a mass of nerves. She kept looking in the rearview mirror, but so far she saw nothing suspicious. It had only been ten minutes since she'd left Cole's house. Mrs. Witherspoon probably hadn't been able to free herself yet, so Amy doubted if Cole knew what had happened. With any luck, it would be hours before he did.

God knew Amy was due a little luck.

Calm down, she told herself.

Just calm down and drive.

A mile later she approached the entrance ramp to I-10 West. Moving into the left lane, she increased speed as she entered the freeway. She wouldn't be able to stay on the interstate long because that would be the first place the authorities would look. But she needed to get a ways out of Mobile before she transferred to secondary roads, so she was taking a calculated risk. She figured the least amount of time she had before Cole called out the dogs was thirty minutes. To be safe, she would then have to move to the smaller highway she had mapped.

Thirty minutes.

Amy stepped on the accelerator and began to pray.

Chapter One

The large blue-and-purple sign loomed on her right, as Amy rounded a bend in the two-lane road.

WELCOME TO MORGAN CREEK, TEXAS
Home of Hathaway Bakery
POPULATION 5,445

Amy was already driving slowly because the road was so narrow, with big ditches on either side. Now she braked to a stop and stared at the sign.

"Hathaway Bakery?" She frowned. Was it possible? Was this Lorna's hometown?

Lorna Hathaway.

Amy hadn't thought of her first college roommate

in years. *Lorna Hathaway*. She had been so nice, so down to earth. If she hadn't casually mentioned her family's business, Amy would never have guessed Lorna came from money. The two girls liked each other immediately and had quickly become friends. But then, at the end of her freshman year, Lorna left Florida State where she'd only enrolled because of her boyfriend and his football scholarship. When the romance soured, she moved back to Texas, transferring to the University of Texas in Austin. Gradually, the girls had lost touch.

Amy looked at the sign again.

Morgan Creek.

Home of Hathaway Bakery...

Somehow, coming upon the sign this way seemed to Amy to be a sign itself. She'd been driving now for eleven straight hours, and she was exhausted, but she'd been uneasy about stopping again. Bad enough she'd had to take a chance on stopping last night. Thank God it had worked out okay. At least, she hoped it had.

She'd chosen a local motel in rural Louisiana. Even though she didn't think Cole could possibly track her down via such a small, out-of-the-way place, she was grateful that the underground network had provided her with Louisiana license plates that she'd put on at the first opportunity. Still, Cole knew what kind of car she drove, and he could provide the authorities with pictures of both her and Calista.

Amy wished she had been able to switch cars—
something that was possible through the network—
but only when you knew ahead of time when you
would be leaving so the arrangements could be made.
Unfortunately, Amy hadn't known, so she'd had no
choice but to use her own car.

Amy was banking on the belief that Cole would
imagine her heading for Florida, where she'd grown
up and where her widower father still lived. She
hoped the first search would concentrate on that area
and give her an edge. Even so, this morning she had
awakened Calista while it was still dark, and they
were on their way again by six.

No sense taking any chances. She wanted as many
miles between her and her ex as she could possibly
get, because new identity or not, if anyone could
track them down, it was Cole.

Hearing a sound from the backseat, Amy turned
around and saw Calista stretching and rubbing her
eyes.

Amy's heart swelled with love. "Hi, sweetie. Did
you have a good nap?"

Calista's forehead knitted into a frown. "Mommy,
I *hungree*." Her bottom lip quivered.

Amy dug into her tote and unearthed a Ziploc bag
filled with Cheerios. She handed it back to her
daughter. "Here you go, pumpkin."

Calista folded her chubby arms across her body in
a familiar pose that signaled impending mutiny. "I

want French fries and a *ham*bugger,'' she said, her frown turning into a thundercloud.

Any other time she'd heard her daughter mangle the word hamburger, Amy would have been amused. Right now she was too tired and too scared to find anything amusing. All she wanted was a safe place to stay. Somewhere she and Calista could get decent food and a clean bed without fear of being found.

''Honeybun, I don't have a hamburger, but as soon as I find a place to stop, we'll get one, I promise.''

Calista started to cry, simultaneously struggling to free herself from her car seat.

Amy wanted to cry, too. Instead, she dropped the bag of Cheerios on the seat next to Calista and, forcing herself to ignore her daughter's tears, headed down the road toward Morgan Creek.

What she would do when she got there, Amy wasn't sure. She only knew she couldn't keep driving indefinitely. She and Calista needed a break or else one or both of them was headed for a meltdown.

Five minutes later she saw the first signs of habitation. Once in the town proper, Amy drove slowly. By the time she'd gone through two stop lights, she'd passed half a dozen storefronts, one bank and two steepled churches—one red brick, one white frame. Spying a service station in the next block on the right, she suddenly knew exactly what she was going to do. She headed for the station. She needed gas, anyway.

The August heat blasted her as she exited the car. By the time she'd extricated Calista from her car seat, Amy's T-shirt was sticking to her.

While the attendant filled her gas tank—Amy had almost forgotten there were still full-service stations in existence—Amy took Calista into the rest room. After washing their hands and faces, Amy combed Calista's hair, as well as her own, then applied fresh lipstick. With Calista in tow, Amy headed into the main building to hunt down a phone book.

"Sure thing, sugar," the dark-eyed woman behind the counter said to Amy's enquiry. Reaching under the counter, she produced a slim, dog-eared directory. "Who would you be lookin' for?"

Amy was taken aback by the woman's question. "Um, just an old friend."

"I know near ever'one in these parts."

Amy hesitated, then realized it was ridiculous to worry about revealing Lorna's name. "This is a girl I knew years ago. I'm not even sure she lives here. Her name is Lorna Hathaway."

"Lorna! Well, sure, sugar, I know Lorna. Shoot, I've known all them Hathaways since they were born." Taking the phone book back from Amy, the woman flipped it open, found the appropriate page, then handed it back. "She's right there," she added, pointing about midway down the right page.

Sure enough, there it was: Hathaway, Lorna. That would never happen in one of the bigger cities.

Women in places like Mobile almost always listed by their initials if they listed at all. When it came to danger, Amy guessed living in a small town was very different from living in a city. Today she was very grateful for that difference.

After paying for her gas, Amy wrote down Lorna's phone number and walked outside to the public phone booth.

Unfortunately, Amy's cell phone could no longer be used, not unless she wanted to take a chance on the call being traced. Would Lorna be there? It was only five-thirty. Maybe she had a job and wouldn't get home until later. The phone at the other end rang six times with no answer. Amy was just about to hang up in disappointment when a breathless voice said, "Hello?"

"Lorna?"

"Yes?"

"Lorna, this is Amy. Amy Summers." Summers was her maiden name. "Do you remember me? From freshman year at Florida State?"

"Amy! I can't believe it. Why, it's been *years*. Of *course* I remember you. Are you still in Florida?"

"Um, actually I'm in the process of moving."

"From Florida?"

"No, from Louisiana."

"That explains it."

"Explains what?"

"Well, last year I was in Orlando for a couple of days, and I thought of you and tried to call you."

"You *did?*" That seemed promising.

"Yes. I was really disappointed not to find you. I even checked with the alumni office at the school, thinking maybe they had an address for you, but they said they didn't."

Amy thought about how Cole had discouraged her from holding on to any part of her old life and how he'd gradually cut her off from everyone and everything he considered a threat to his total domination of her. He had even tried to keep her from visiting her father, but in that, Amy had put her foot down.

"So where are you now?" Lorna asked.

"Actually, I'm right here. In Morgan Creek."

"You *are?*"

"I don't blame you for being surprised." Amy grimaced. "It's a long story. I'm just traveling through, but I was hoping we might be able to get together." She mentally crossed her fingers. "I thought I'd try to find a hotel around here, at least for tonight."

"I'd *love* to get together. And forget about finding a hotel. You're staying with me. I've got tons of room. Oh, Amy, I'm so thrilled you called! Okay, where, exactly, are you?"

Amy told her, and Lorna quickly gave her directions to her place. "It's the third house on the right-hand side of the street. You can't miss it. A yellow Victorian with dark-brown trim.''

Just as Lorna said, Amy had no trouble finding her street or the house. It was lovely—a beautifully kept, gingerbready Victorian with a cupola and a wrap-around porch filled with wicker furniture and even a porch swing. What a perfect house, yet it seemed far too big for just one person. Though Lorna's name had been listed in the directory as Hathaway, Amy wondered if she might be married, and if she had children.

Amy parked her silver Toyota on the street in front of the house and had barely gotten her driver's-side door open when Lorna came bounding out the front door and down the porch steps.

Amy would have recognized her old friend anywhere. Lorna was older, yes, but she was still slender and blond, although her hair, which used to be halfway down her back, was now worn much shorter, in one of those messy styles currently popular. Amy, whose own dark hair was wildly curly, would have loved to pull off that more sophisticated look but knew it would never be in the cards.

"Amy!" Lorna's smile was huge, her bright-blue eyes sparkling with excitement. Before Amy could open the back door to retrieve Calista, Lorna had enveloped her in an exuberant hug. "Oh, it's wonderful to see you." Releasing Amy, she stood back and studied her. "You look great. Not a day older than the last time I saw you."

Amy made a face. "You never were a good liar. I look terrible and I know it."

"You couldn't look terrible if you tried."

"Mom*mee!*"

Lorna's eyes widened and she stooped down to look into the car. "And who's this precious little one?"

"That's Calista, my daughter. Here, let me get her out."

Lorna stood back to allow Amy to free Calista from her car seat. Calista stared at Lorna curiously as Amy lifted her out of the car.

"Well, hello, Calista," Lorna said. "Aren't you a pretty girl?"

Calista, who even at three loved compliments, grinned, revealing the deep dimples she'd inherited from Amy's mother.

"Oh, Amy, she's beautiful."

Amy couldn't help noticing the wistful note in Lorna's voice. While continuing to coo over Calista, Lorna helped Amy gather her belongings. Then the three headed up the walkway to the house.

Amy wished she could properly appreciate the well-cared-for lawn and the abundance of colorful summer flowers and shrubs surrounding the house, but she was too on edge to truly enjoy anything but the possibility of at least one night's respite from worry.

The house felt wonderfully cool in contrast to the heat outdoors and smelled of lemon furniture polish. A quick look around the entry hall revealed shining hardwood floors, beautiful antiques and gorgeous carpets, that gave her an overall impression of both good taste and charm. A fan whirred softly overhead.

"The house is actually clean, thank goodness," Lorna said. "I have a woman who comes in twice a week, and today was one of her days."

"It's lovely." It was more than lovely. It was tranquil. Amy immediately felt less nervous and frightened just being there. It was as if nothing bad could possibly happen to her—to *them*—in a house this peaceful.

"Before I show you around, shall we take your things upstairs to the guest room?"

"This is so nice of you, Lorna."

Lorna made a disparaging gesture. "Hey, we're friends. Besides, I'm so *excited* to have you!"

"Well, I really appreciate it."

Lorna took one of the suitcases and the tote Amy'd had in the car, then led the way up the graceful, curved staircase to the right of the entry hall. Upstairs she showed Amy to a large front bedroom that overlooked the street.

"Oh, it's beautiful," Amy said. The walls were covered with a creamy wallpaper in an old-fashioned

pattern of big pink cabbage roses and garlands of ivy.
It was charming and reminded Amy of the wallpaper
that used to be in her grandmother's bedroom. The
furnishings were just as charming: a four-poster bed
with a pale-green comforter and matching dust ruffle,
a walnut chest of drawers and armoire, a desk and
accompanying chair, and best of all, a wide window
seat covered with a thick green pillow. A large teddy
bear sat on it.

"Bear!" Calista pointed, eyes wide.

"Oh, dear," Amy said as Calista immediately
headed for the stuffed animal.

Lorna smiled, watching her. "She can play with
the bear. It's a holdover from when my nieces were
little."

"Calista can be kind of rough with her toys."

"Doesn't matter." Turning back to Amy, she
added, "I'm sorry, but I don't have a crib for her. I
do have a cot, though."

"Calista doesn't sleep in a crib anymore, anyway."

"If you don't want the cot, she can have a room
of her own, whichever you think is best."

"She can just sleep with me."

"Are you sure?"

Amy smiled. "I'm sure. That's what we would
have done if we'd gotten a hotel. This is perfect."

"All right. Why don't I leave you two alone for
a little while, then? You can unpack your things

while I make a phone call, okay? Then we can start catching up."

"Okay."

When Lorna had gone back downstairs, Amy sank onto the bed and let Calista explore the room. What she wouldn't give to be able to remain here for a couple of days, but she knew she couldn't afford to overstay her welcome. If Lorna should offer, that would be one thing. But Amy couldn't ask.

While Calista played contentedly with the stuffed animal, talking her own version of "bear" talk to him, Amy unpacked their night clothes. It was probably pointless to take anything else out of the suitcases, since in all probability she would be on the road again in the morning, but she did take clean shorts and tops out for both of them to wear tomorrow.

"Okay, sweetie, time to say bye-bye to Bear."

Calista gave her a dark look, shaking her head and hugging the bear tighter.

Amy sighed. "Oh, all right. You can take Bear downstairs."

As the two slowly descended the stairs, Amy heard Lorna saying goodbye to someone, and by the time they reached the entry, Lorna had come out to meet them.

"Are either of you hungry? We won't be having dinner until seven-thirty or later, but I have cheese and crackers and fruit we could have now."

"I know Calista's hungry," Amy said, praying that her daughter wouldn't turn her nose up at the snack and start demanding a hamburger again.

"Let's go back to the kitchen, then."

The kitchen was exactly what Amy would have expected it to be: big, bright and cheerful—done in pale yellow with red accents—and dominated by a fireplace at one end and a big, round oak table in the center. Looking like a Currier & Ives print, the fireplace was flanked on one side by an oak rocking chair and on the other by a fat calico cat who eyed them as they entered the room.

"Kitty!" Calista shouted, immediately racing over to the feline.

"Calista, don't touch the cat," Amy said, rushing after her daughter. "Sometimes cats scratch."

"It's okay," Lorna said. "Buttercup is an unusual cat. She actually *likes* little kids."

And she did seem to, Amy saw, because when Calista reached out to pet the cat's head, Buttercup actually leaned into the caress, and Amy heard her purr.

Calista laughed delightedly and sat down on the hearth next to the cat. Amy watched for a while, but quickly realized she didn't need to worry.

"Can I help you?" she asked Lorna.

"Thanks, but there's nothing much to do. Just have a seat."

Within minutes the table was laden with the cheese

and crackers, a bunch of red seedless grapes and a wedge of some kind of paté that looked wonderful.

"Milk for Calista?" she asked.

"Please."

"I've even got a sip cup left from my nieces."

"Great."

It took some doing to get Calista away from Buttercup, but after promising her if she ate everything, she could play with the cat again, she came to the table. Once she was happily eating, the two friends finally had a chance to talk.

"Before we start filling in what's happened since we last saw each other," Lorna said, "I just wanted to give you a heads-up. Tonight there's a dinner party being given at my family's home to celebrate my grandmother's ninetieth birthday, and you and Calista are invited to come, too."

"Oh, no, we couldn't," Amy said. "You go on and don't worry about us. We'll just find something to eat in town somewhere."

"There's no way I'm letting you 'find something to eat' while I go off to a party."

"It's not like you invited us to come," Amy pointed out. "We practically invited ourselves. I don't want you changing your plans because of us."

"Look, I'm not leaving you here alone. I called the house and told my grandmother about you, and she insisted I bring you along tonight. She said it would be the height of rudeness to leave a guest

home alone while I went out to dinner," Lorna
grinned. "Believe me, when Grandmother Stella is-
sues a command, a good Hathaway obeys."

Amy had to admit she was curious about Lorna's
family, especially her grandmother, whom Lorna had
mentioned more than once in that year they'd been
roommates. But tonight was such a special occasion,
and Amy and Calista were outsiders. It just didn't
seem right for them to be taking part in a family
celebration.

"Now, we only have about an hour until we have
to start getting ready. Grandmother's a stickler for
punctuality and tonight's shindig starts at seven...so
let's quit wasting time arguing about whether you're
coming with me or not and let's catch up."

In the next twenty minutes Amy learned that Lorna
had come back to Morgan Creek after getting her
master's degree and had worked in the family business ever since. She had been married, she said, but
was now divorced, and had no children. This last had
been relayed matter-of-factly, but Lorna couldn't disguise the longing she obviously felt. It was there
every time she looked at Calista, and Amy felt bad
for her friend. Calista was the light of her life, the
best thing that had ever happened to her—despite the
fact she'd had to be married to Cole to get her—and
Amy felt sorry for everyone who hadn't experienced
that same joy, especially when it was so obvious they
wanted children.

"Now let's hear everything about you," Lorna said when she'd finished.

Amy looked over at Calista.

Lorna immediately nodded. "Calista, would you like to play with Buttercup in the backyard? She needs to get some exercise."

Calista grinned. "Yeah!"

"We can sit on the back porch and watch her," Lorna said to Amy.

Once they were settled outside—with Calista playing happily and out of earshot, Amy felt free to talk.

"Like you, I'm divorced. My ex lives in Shreveport. He's an investment banker." Neither was true. Cole was a high-powered lawyer turned politician and he lived in Mobile, but Amy knew from the women in the underground network that she couldn't afford to take any chances or trust anyone, no matter who, and had rehearsed the story she would tell to everyone from now on.

"He never really wanted children," she continued, "so he didn't object when I decided to head for the West Coast where I understand teachers—even preschool teachers like me—make really good money." This was partially true. Cole *hadn't* wanted children. After all, how could he remain the center of Amy's universe if he had to share her with a child? But he would have objected violently to Amy's leaving Mobile with Calista if he'd known about it. Not because he cared about Calista, but because he knew Amy did.

The divorce had infuriated Cole. He'd fought Amy every step of the way. Where she'd gotten the strength to actually leave him and file for divorce, she'd never know, because Cole had beaten her down so much over the years, it had always been easier to just go along with whatever it was he wanted than to actually assert herself.

To retaliate and hurt her in the worst possible way, he had produced "witnesses" who swore under oath that they had seen Amy doing drugs and neglecting Calista. Because of Cole's position and the friends who lied for him, he was given custody of Calista, and Amy was only allowed to see her twice a week under strict supervision.

"So you're a teacher?" Lorna said. "I thought you were a journalism major."

"I was, briefly. But during the summer between my freshman year and my sophomore year, I worked at a day-care center. I loved working with kids so much, I decided to switch to early childhood education. Up until I got married, I taught kindergarten."

"Up until you got married?"

Amy nodded. "My ex didn't want me to work." Seeing the look on Lorna's face, Amy added wryly, "How could I focus all my time and energy on *him* if I was working?"

Lorna made a face. "Oh. *That* kind of man."

Amy shuddered. "You have no idea."

"And yet he was okay with you moving and taking Calista with you?"

"He didn't have a choice."

Lorna nodded. "How long were you married?"

"Seven years. Seven *long* years. How about you?"

"Six years."

"What happened? If you don't mind my asking?"

"A twenty-year-old Dallas Cowboys cheerleader with big boobs."

"Oh, Lorna, that stinks."

Lorna shrugged. "The bloom was off the rose by then, anyway. I realized early on I'd made a bad mistake, but I hung on stubbornly, thinking I could make it work if I just tried hard enough. Thing is, it takes two, and Keith wasn't trying. He was looking for greener pastures…or should I say someone more adoring than I was ever going to be."

"Were you living here in Morgan Creek when this happened?"

"Uh-huh. And that may have been a big part of the problem. He hated working for my family, but more than that, he really hated that I had more say-so in the running of the company than he did. Keith has to be top dog and he wasn't." She shrugged. "I don't know. Maybe if I'd loved him more, I would have tried harder to make him happy. It wasn't all his fault." For a moment she was silent. Then she smiled and lifted her glass of lemonade. "But that's water under the bridge. Now here we are, two women who have learned some tough lessons but who are cutting their losses and moving on. To survival!"

Amy clinked her glass against Lorna's. "To survival."

Chapter Two

Bryce Hathaway wasn't looking forward to the evening. Although his family had always made a big deal out of birthdays, especially those of his grandmother, Stella, the oldest living Hathaway, he knew tonight's celebration would be a trial because Stella Morgan Hathaway had been on the warpath for the past week.

The reason was Bryce's youngest sister, Claudia. Since earning her MBA, Claudia had worked in the family business, but it was apparent to everyone that, unlike Lorna, she hated it. With Bryce's encouragement, Claudia had begun to investigate other job opportunities. This meant there was a high probability

she would be leaving Morgan Creek since there were
few other job prospects in this town for someone like
Claudia outside of Hathaway Bakery. But the truth
was, part of the reason Claudia disliked working for
the family business was the fact it was in Morgan
Creek, as Bryce well knew.

Bryce couldn't blame his youngest sister for the
way she felt. As she'd put it last week, what were
her chances of finding a guy she might want to spend
her life with if she stayed in what she called "this
one-horse town"? Bryce knew the answer: slim to
none.

Hence Grandmother Stella's displeasure, which
was now aimed not only at Claudia but at Bryce
himself.

Bryce grimaced. On top of having to contend with
his grandmother's dark looks and heavy disapproval,
there was also the immediate problem of a nanny for
his daughters. The second one in less than six months
had abruptly quit the previous Friday. Bryce guessed
he understood why it was so hard for him to keep a
nanny. Claudia wasn't the only educated woman who
didn't want to be stuck in a small town like Morgan
Creek. And even if these women didn't mind the
town, they *did* mind the six-days-a-week, live-in re-
quirements of the job. Not even the generous salary
and private suite of rooms seemed to make up for
these negatives.

Plus there was Susan.

Bryce knew he should be angry with his younger daughter, but it was hard for him to stay mad at Susan, no matter how far she tested his patience, because she was so vibrant and full of life. In those dark months after Michelle's death, Susan had been the only one who could make Bryce smile and forget his pain.

But the nannies employed since the death of his wife three years earlier weren't as forgiving of Susan's pranks and subtle forms of torture as he was. Even Stella's sweetness couldn't make up for her younger sister's hijinks and sometimes aggravating behavior, as one recent nanny had told Bryce in exasperation.

"I've had all I can take," the woman had said.

"Look, I'm sorry about the lizard—"

"Yes," she'd said, "I'm sure you are, but I'm still leaving."

The lizard in the jewelry box was only the latest in a series of calculated attempts to get the nanny to resign. Susan had made no bones about the fact she didn't like Miss Reynolds, and no matter what kind of punishment he exacted, he also knew Susan would never change. Until he found a nanny she liked, she would continue to drive them away.

"Daddy, I'm ready."

Bryce blinked, then smiled down at Stella. It always amused him that his grandmother's namesake was totally unlike her in temperament, whereas Susan personified the phrase "chip off the old block."

"And where is your sister?"

"She'll be here in a minute. She's fixing her hair."

Stella's own hair, a rich golden brown like Bryce's, lay in perfect waves held neatly back from her face with a coral headband that matched her coral sundress. Around her neck was a strand of coral beads.

"You look very nice, honey."

Stella ducked her head in shy pleasure. "Thank you."

"I hope your sister has taken the trouble to look good for your grandmother, too."

Before Stella could respond, Susan came racing down the stairs—hair flying, face flushed, eyes immediately zeroing in on Stella's.

Bryce knew that look. Susan was up to something she knew he would disapprove of and was silently commanding her sister to keep her mouth shut. He also knew it would be futile to question either girl. Whatever it was Susan was planning, he'd just have to wait until it happened. Then he would deal with her.

He quickly inspected Susan, who—miracle of miracles—had chosen to wear a green flowered sundress just as pretty as Stella's. Even her curlier hair—a shade lighter than Stella's—looked good.

Bryce smiled his approval. "All right. Let's gather

up your grandmother's presents and get going. You know how she feels about people not being on time.''

Susan made a face, then grinned at Stella.

Stella returned Susan's smile.

Sometimes it pained Bryce to see how much Stella wanted to please—not just him, but everyone. He hoped she would outgrow this tendency and become more independent in her thinking. Otherwise he was afraid she was bound to have lots of problems in life, not to mention the very real possibility that she might decide she needed to please the wrong people. He knew he would have to keep close tabs on her, maybe even closer tabs than on Susan.

It was damned hard being a parent, and being a single parent was even worse, especially to daughters. Good thing he had three younger sisters. At least he had a better understanding of girls and the way their minds worked than a man who had never been around many females.

Even so, it was tough raising the girls on his own. He never knew if he was doing the right thing or not. Most of the time, he just muddled through each day and prayed for the best.

Thank God for Lorna, he thought as he and the girls walked across the park-like land that separated his home from the family mansion and gave at least an illusion of privacy. His favorite sister had no children of her own and, especially since her divorce and Michelle's death, had lavished her motherly instincts and attention on his daughters. They, in turn, adored their aunt Lorna.

The lights of the big house, as Bryce and his siblings had always referred to the main residence within the family compound, were ablaze as he and the children approached.

"Daddy? Is Cameron going to be here tonight?"

"Yes, Susan, everyone's going to be here."

"Cool."

Cameron was the daughter of Bryce's sister Chloe and her husband Greg, who lived in Austin. Although Cameron was fourteen, six years older than Stella and seven years older than Susan, they both worshiped her. At the moment, she was their only Hathaway cousin, and the way things were going, Bryce was sorely afraid that situation wouldn't change anytime soon. He knew Lorna had wanted children when she was married but had had some medical problems. Now, of course, she was no longer married. And Chloe didn't seem inclined to have another, either. Claudia was their only hope.

By now they'd reached the wide, shallow steps leading to the massive oak double front door, which was flanked by flickering gas lamps. Although this was the house where Bryce had grown up, he never entered without either knocking or ringing the doorbell, a courtesy he expected to be returned when any member of his family visited him.

The door was promptly opened by Lucy, one of

the maids. "Good evenin', Mr. Bryce." She gave him a big smile, then looked down at the girls. "And Miss Susan and Miss Stella. My, don't you two girls look pretty?"

"Good evening, Lucy." Bryce nudged the girls, who politely said their hellos and thank-yous.

"Everyone is in the drawing room," Lucy announced.

Bryce mentally rolled his eyes. Calling the living room the drawing room was something his mother had initiated a few years back, after a trip to England. The affectation had always bothered him. The Hathaways made no pretense of being upper class. Like the Morgans, his grandmother's family, the Hathaways had come from hardy pioneer stock—people who had worked hard for a living, doing mostly physical work.

Why his mother felt the need to pretend otherwise was a mystery to him. But it hadn't seemed worth making an issue of, just as so many things were not worth causing more strife in the family than was already there. Bryce believed in picking his battles carefully. That way, his energy was channeled into areas that were important and not just irritations.

The girls raced ahead of him into the large rectangular room that took up the entire right front section of the house. An equally large dining room was across the hall, occupying the left front of the house.

As he entered the elegantly furnished room, he realized most of his family had already arrived. Lorna stood talking to a petite, dark-haired woman Bryce didn't know, and there was Chloe, her husband Greg and their daughter Cameron, who had all driven down from Austin, and of course Claudia, who still lived at home, along with Bryce's parents, Jonathan and Kathleen.

Before stopping to talk to anyone else, he headed straight for the far end of the room where his grandmother sat ensconced in a navy velvet Queen Anne chair. At ninety, Stella Morgan Hathaway was still a handsome woman with regal bearing. Her snowy, waist-length hair had been twisted and piled on top of her head, secured with diamond and ruby combs. Matching diamond and ruby earrings and bracelet glittered in her ears and on her right wrist. She wore a long, garnet satin evening dress and, to guard against the chill of the air-conditioning, a white cashmere shawl was draped around her shoulders.

As Bryce and the girls approached, she lifted her chin. Although she smiled, her blue eyes were cool as they met his.

Still mad at me, he thought. His answering smile was warm and loving, for he *did* love his imperious, stubborn grandmother. He'd always loved her. When he was a boy, she was the one he confided in, the one who counseled him and comforted him and encouraged him. His mother had been too preoccupied with the social activities she used as a substitute for a happy marriage, and his father had been too mired in his own insecurities and discontent to spend much time or effort on his son.

The girls hugged and kissed their great-grandmother, added their presents to the pile near her feet, then skipped off to join their cousin.

Bryce bent down and kissed his grandmother's soft cheek. The scent of roses, a hallmark of her favorite perfume, clung to her skin. "Happy birthday, Grandmother."

"It would be a lot happier if you would talk some sense into Claudia."

"Gran, we've been all through this."

Her lips tightened. "That doesn't mean I'm satisfied with your decision."

"I know, and I'm sorry about that." Bryce almost added more, then decided not to. As he'd pointed out, everything had already been said. More than once. He wasn't going to change his mind, and his grandmother would not change hers. "We'll just have to agree to disagree."

"I suppose you approve of that application she made to that school in Houston."

"Yes, I do." Claudia had applied to teach business classes at a community college there.

"Hmmph. Houston. Nothing but dirt and crime and traffic."

"Gran, that's not true. I've been to Houston lots of times, and I really like the city. There's lots of energy there. And lots of young people. If a job comes through for Claudia, I think it'll be good for her to move there.''

He could see how his grandmother was struggling not to lose her temper. This issue was one of the few times Bryce had ever crossed her, one of the few times *anyone* had ever crossed her, and he knew his opposition was hard for her to swallow.

Saying, ''You've ruined my birthday,'' she put her chin in the air and refused to utter another word.

Giving her a second kiss on the cheek, he murmured, ''I'm sorry you feel that way, Gran. Try to remember that disagreeing with you doesn't mean I don't love you.'' Turning away, he finally directed his attention to the other guests in the room.

''Bryce,'' Lorna said. She had walked up behind him with the stranger he'd noticed earlier in tow. ''I'd like you to meet an old friend. Amy, this is my brother, Bryce. Bryce, this is Amy—'' Lorna broke off and gave her friend a quizzical smile. ''I never asked you what your married name is. Or if you had gone back to using Summers again?''

''Not with Calista,'' the woman said. ''Our last name is Gordon.''

''Oh, of course. I took *my* maiden name back because there weren't any children involved.''

Bryce took this exchange to mean the woman was divorced.

Turning her attention back to him, Lorna said,

"Amy and I met at Florida State that year I was there. In fact, we were roommates. She and her little girl are staying with me for a few days." She inclined her head. "That's Calista over there, with Cameron and the girls."

Bryce caught a glimpse of a cute, dark-haired girl in a pink-checked dress.

"It's nice to meet you, Amy," he said, wondering when they had arrived. Lorna hadn't mentioned expecting company at work today.

"Thank you." Amy smiled and put her hand out.

Bryce shook it. She had a firm grip for such a small woman. She also had a direct gaze and huge brown eyes that dominated her face. "I hope you won't be bored here. There's not much to do in Morgan Creek."

"It'll be fun just to catch up with Lorna."

He liked her voice, too. It was low, with a musical quality and slight Southern drawl. "So you two were roommates?" Those eyes really were incredible. It wasn't just their size. Their color—a rich, warm brown flecked with gold—was arresting, and setting them off were thick dark lashes.

"Yes. And I missed Lorna after she left."

She smiled at Lorna, and Bryce saw that she had a small dimple at the right side of her mouth.

"Amy's on her way to California," Lorna explained. "She's a kindergarten teacher and hopes to find a job and settle out there."

"Whereabouts in California?"

Amy shrugged. "I don't know for sure. I like small towns, and I was thinking maybe I'd go somewhere near the San Diego area."

As Bryce was framing another question, a flurry at the entrance to the living room announced another arrival. Bryce saw that it was Jake Kenyon, their neighbor and a long-time family friend, accompanied by his daughter, Tara. Tara and Bryce had grown up together, and until Bryce had met and fallen in love with Michelle, Bryce knew that his family and most of the townspeople had assumed he and Tara would eventually marry.

Tara had married within six months of Bryce, and Bryce had always wondered if the marriage had been her answer to his. Whatever the reason, it hadn't lasted long. Not even two years, and the union had produced no children.

During the years Bryce was married to Michelle, Tara had spent most of her time in Dallas, working as a runway model for several of the designers based in the city. She hadn't needed to work—as Jake's only child she had plenty of money and stood to inherit a fortune—but Bryce knew the attention she received from her modeling and the whirl of the Dallas social scene were the big draws. At one point, she'd been engaged to some bigshot Dallas power broker, but she'd broken the engagement. He'd never known the reason why.

Six months ago she'd returned to Morgan Creek and now spent her time helping her father with his many business interests. She'd also become heavily involved with the local rodeo committee, for Morgan Creek and the neighboring town of Bailey Springs joined together to sponsor the annual Morgan Bailey Livestock Show and Rodeo, one of the largest in Texas.

Bryce genuinely liked Tara, and sometimes he wondered if that affection and their long friendship and similar backgrounds might not be enough...for something more. The girls seemed to like her, too. And yet...after having the real thing with Michelle he wasn't sure he could settle for less.

With this thought in mind, he watched as Tara and her father headed in his direction.

Tara Kenyon looked like a movie star, Amy thought. Tall and slim at about five foot eight, she had luxurious chestnut hair and glittering green eyes. Her features were flawless: straight nose neither too long nor too short, plump lips, perfect white teeth, beautifully arched brows, long, thick, curly eyelashes and a creamy complexion with just a hint of a tan.

And that body! Amy could only dream of such a body. It was very slender yet curvy, with full high breasts and a nicely rounded rear.

Tonight she wore a figure-skimming silk sheath in a shade of tangerine that looked fabulous on her and complemented both her hair and her skin. The dress ended several inches above her knees, revealing long, gorgeous legs and high arched feet with perfectly manicured toes shown to advantage in strappy gold stiletto heels.

Next to her, Amy felt colorless and dull in her beige dress and plain brown sandals, but the outfit was the best she'd packed in readiness for her chance to flee. The reminder that she was here on false pretenses took away some of the pleasure she'd begun to feel at her warm welcome from Lorna's family.

Watching Tara, Amy saw that she acted like a star, too, barely acknowledging the introduction to Amy as her gaze moved unerringly to Bryce. Only then did she turn on the full wattage of her smile.

Leaning forward, she kissed him on the mouth. "Hello, stranger. Haven't seen you in a few days," she drawled sweetly. "Where have you been hiding yourself?"

"Another nanny quit," Bryce said.

"Are you sure you're not beating them or something? Not that it might not be pleasant to be beaten by you." This last was said with a low chuckle.

With unspoken accord, Amy and Lorna moved away.

"Bitch," Lorna muttered.

Amy couldn't help laughing. "I take it you don't like her?" she whispered.

"Remind me to tell you some Tara stories tonight after we get back to the house."

Just then Lorna's youngest sister, Claudia, approached. Amy had met Claudia and the rest of Lorna's family earlier and was struck by how attractive they all were. Lorna reminded Amy of Cameron Diaz with her big eyes and wide smile, whereas Claudia was a Meg Ryan type with her coltish grace and impish grin. Chloe, the oldest sister, had more classical good looks, sort of a cross between a young Cheryl Ladd or a Michelle Pfeiffer. They were all blonde—although Amy suspected some of the blond came from a bottle—blue-eyed, slender and tanned.

Bryce was very attractive, too, but in a different way. His hair was darker than the girls'—more brown than blond—but he also had those intense blue Hathaway eyes. Amy decided she wouldn't exactly call him handsome. His chin was too square and his nose a tad crooked, but in addition to those great eyes, he had a terrific smile, and he exuded warmth and strength. Not to mention tons of sex appeal. These were all qualities Amy was sure most women found irresistible—not just Tara Kenyon.

It was easy to see where the women got their good looks, for their mother, Kathleen, was a beauty, almost as perfectly put together in her way as Tara Kenyon was in hers. Yet there was something about the expression in Kathleen Hathaway's eyes that told Amy the older woman wasn't happy. Amy wondered if that unhappiness was related to Lorna's father. Jonathan Hathaway was handsome, but there was a softness about him that Amy found off-putting.

"So what are you two plotting?" Claudia asked with a grin as she joined them.

"No plot," Lorna said. She leaned over and stage-whispered into Claudia's ear, "Just dissing Miss T."

Claudia grimaced. "Oh. Her."

Amy was gratified to find she wasn't alone in her almost immediate dislike of Tara Kenyon. Glancing back, she saw that the woman had slipped her arm through Bryce's and was looking up at him as if he were the only person in the room.

"Yep," Lorna said, following Amy's gaze. "She's gunning for him."

"Your brother doesn't act as if he minds." It disappointed Amy that he seemed to welcome Tara's attentions, but it didn't surprise her. No man would be immune to a woman like Tara, she was afraid.

"She's been after Bryce since she was knee high to a grasshopper," Claudia said with an exaggerated country accent.

"Yeah, she nearly croaked when he brought Michelle home and announced their engagement," Lorna added with a wicked grin. "I don't think it ever entered her head that he'd marry someone else. It's one of the few times in Tara's life that she's ever been denied something she coveted."

Just then Bryce and Tara walked in their direction, and the sisters immediately changed the subject.

"So, Amy," Claudia said, "Lorna tells us you're heading to California?"

Amy nodded.

"Do you have family out there?"

"No. I just wanted a change."

"She wanted to get away from her ex," Lorna added.

"Well, I admire you. I want a change, too, but I haven't done much about it."

"You're doing something," Lorna said.

"Finally," Claudia said.

"Hey, it's not easy bucking Gran."

Claudia made a face. "Tell me about it."

"Mommy, Mommy! Lookit what I got."

The three women turned at the sound of Calista's excited voice. Amy smiled as her daughter, followed by Bryce's two girls, skidded to a stop in front of her. Eyes bright with happiness, she lifted a strand of coral beads that were hanging around her neck.

"Where did you get those?" Amy asked.

"Stelwa gave 'em to me."

Stella Hathaway gave Amy a shy smile.

"That was sweet of you, Stella," Lorna said. She pulled Stella close and gave her a shoulder hug.

"I have some beads like those," Susan piped up, "but mine are green. She can have mine, too."

It was obvious from her tone of voice that Susan had no intention of being outdone by her sister.

"What generous girls you are." This came from Claudia, who winked at Amy.

"Did you say thank you?" Amy asked Calista.

"Uh-huh."

"Well, I'd like to thank you girls, too." Amy smiled down at Susan and Stella. "But maybe your father won't like you giving away your jewelry."

Susan made a face. "He doesn't care."

"We bought the beads with our own money," Stella offered. "When we were in Mexico last year."

"You went to Mexico?" Amy said.

"Uh-huh," Susan said. "We took a cruise with Daddy."

"That sounds like fun."

"Claudia and I went, too," Lorna said. "And it *was* fun."

"We had our own party," Susan said.

"While the adults were having a cocktail party," Lorna explained.

"It was cool," Stella said. "We got to dance and everything."

They talked about the cruise a few more minutes, then the girls trooped off—the older two each holding one of Calista's hands.

"I haven't seen those girls take to anyone like that in a long time," Claudia said, watching them walk away.

"Neither have I," Lorna added thoughtfully.

Amy watched them, too, thinking how much she was going to hate leaving Morgan Creek. She'd only been here a few hours and already she felt at home. And, obviously, so did Calista. It really was sweet how Susan and Stella were looking after her.

Just then one of the maids came around with a tray holding glasses of champagne, and a few minutes later the adults were called across to the dining room where dinner was ready to be served. The children would eat in the morning room, Lorna explained to Amy, supervised by two teenage sitters her mother had hired for the evening. "Mother and Gran like civilized meals," she added with a laugh. "Meaning, they don't even want to *see* the children, let alone hear them."

"Yeah," Claudia said. "We weren't allowed to dine with the adults until we turned sixteen. And even then, woe to anyone who couldn't behave themselves."

Amy thought about the way she was raised, which was so different. Of course, she was an only child and had been born to parents who were already in their forties and who had never expected to have a child. Consequently, they were so delighted, they liked having her with them all the time. When Amy started school, it was Amy's mother who had cried instead of Amy. Remembering, Amy felt a frisson of sadness. Her mother had been dead for nearly ten years, and Amy still missed her.

Once in the dining room, Amy found herself seated across the table from Tara Kenyon and Bryce, who was on Tara's right. Amy was seated between Lorna and Greg Standish, Chloe's husband. Greg was extremely handsome, Amy thought, and very charming. Almost too charming. When he turned to her, giving her the full force of his attention, she decided if he were *her* husband, she might never let him out the door.

"So you and Lorna were roommates in college?" he said.

"Yes."

"Lucky Lorna," he murmured.

Amy had never been comfortable with men who flirted as easily as they breathed. She was not a mistress of light banter, and she was particularly bad at anything with sexual overtones. Maybe this was because she had spent her working life with children, who were nothing if not direct, so she'd never had a chance to master subtleties. Or maybe it was because Cole had been so possessive and jealous that she'd had no opportunities to develop her skill at casual, social flirting. On the other hand, maybe it just wasn't in her to be anything but straightforward in her relationships with others. And yet, here she was, presenting a false front to all these nice people, she thought with a renewed stab of guilt.

"Behave yourself, Greg," Lorna said.

Greg just laughed and winked at Amy.

"Bryce," Lorna said, "did you notice how taken Susan and Stella are with Amy's little girl?"

"I did." His gaze met Amy's, and he smiled. "She's a charmer."

"Thank you."

"Well behaved, too," Lorna added. "Which isn't surprising, seeing as how Amy's background is teaching young children. I think I told you that's what she plans to do in California."

Amy wished she could find a way to change the subject. She was sure Lorna's brother didn't care what her plans were, plus she didn't like being the focus of everyone's attention.

"Why are you going to California?" Bryce asked. "Is it because you have a job lined up there?"

She knew he was just being polite. "No, not yet."

"Would you consider staying in Texas if you could find a job here?"

She was surprised by the question. "I…I don't know. I hadn't thought about it. I guess if I happened upon a job somewhere like Morgan Creek, I would. I like small towns."

Bryce studied her for a long moment. She couldn't imagine what he was thinking.

Then he said, "Maybe that could be arranged."

"Really? Do you know of an opening here?"

He nodded slowly. "Yes, I do."

At this, Tara Kenyon said, "She's a *kindergarten* teacher, Bryce. There's only one kindergarten in Morgan Creek, and Allison Stuckey has that job."

"I was thinking along different lines," Bryce said, not looking at Tara. Once again he smiled. "Amy, what would you think about coming to work for me as a live-in nanny to my girls?"

Chapter Three

Amy's mouth dropped open. "Wh-what did you say?"

"I said, how would you like to work for me as a live-in nanny to my girls?"

As Amy digested this startling development, she realized this offer might be the answer to her prayers. Cole would never look for her in Morgan Creek because he wasn't even aware of its existence or the fact she had any connection to it. Working for Bryce would mean she would be living on this compound, behind high walls with a sophisticated security system, to all intents and purposes hidden from view.

She and Calista would be safe.

"Bryce, being a nanny isn't like teaching school," Tara said.

Ignoring Tara's remark, Bryce kept his attention trained on Amy. "It seems to me we could help each other out. I need someone young and energetic and experienced with children to supervise my girls. And you need a job and a way to care for your daughter at the same time. This would solve both our problems. I'll make it worth your while and pay you as much as you'd make teaching." He named a generous amount.

Tara had no intention of being ignored. "Have you any experience with girls the ages of Stella and Susan?" she said.

Her voice was perfectly pleasant and reasonable, but Amy knew the woman was not pleased. "Actually," Amy answered just as pleasantly, "I have." She turned to Bryce again. "I'm certified to teach kindergarten through second grade, and even though most of my experience is with kindergarten, I did substitute teach in both first and second grades my first year out of college."

He nodded, obviously pleased. "Stella just completed second grade, and Susan will begin second grade this year."

"I figured as much," Amy said.

"So what do you say? Interested in the job?"

"Oh, Amy, it would be great to have you here!" Lorna said. "Please say yes."

Although Amy was so thrilled about the job offer she wanted to get up and dance around the room, she managed to reply calmly and in a businesslike manner. "I appreciate your confidence in me, and I accept your offer. I promise I won't let you down."

"Great," Bryce said.

"Oh, I'm so excited!" Lorna said.

Amy stole another glance at Tara. Although she still maintained an even expression, her eyes as they met Amy's were as cold and hard as Bryce's were warm and welcoming.

Amy suddenly had that feeling her mother used to describe as "someone walking over my grave." She knew as certainly as she knew her own name that she had made an enemy in Tara Kenyon, who obviously viewed her as some kind of threat. Why this should be so, Amy had no idea. After all, Tara was beautiful and rich and from the same social class as Bryce, whereas she, Amy, was not beautiful or rich and certainly not even close to the same class of people as the Hathaways.

She wanted to say, *Chill, honey, I'm just the hired help. Your claim on Bryce Hathaway is perfectly safe. He would no more be interested in me than one of the maids.*

Sure, Bryce liked her. She could see he liked her. But his liking her had to do with his children and his need for someone to take care of them and not to anything else. Amy was enough of a realist to know that. Anyway, even if Bryce *did* like her in another way, it wouldn't make any difference. Amy wasn't interested in romance. Not yet. Maybe never. And even if she *were,* how could she get involved with any man under false pretenses? The fact was, she was living a lie, and a lie was no basis upon which to form a serious relationship.

For the rest of the meal, Tara managed to dominate Bryce's attention, and Amy knew it was no fluke that she did it talking about people, events and subjects Amy knew nothing about and couldn't possibly comment on. Amy was amused. Tara thought she was effectively cutting Amy out, but she was actually doing her a favor, because now Amy could try to relax and just enjoy her dinner.

Even so, she was relieved when dinner was finally over and she could escape the table. Grinning, Lorna linked her arm with Amy's as they headed toward the morning room and the children.

"I'm so tickled you're going to be staying on," she said. "It'll be such fun to have you here."

"I'm pleased, too. It was really nice of your brother to offer me the job."

"Hey, you're doing him a favor. He's had a devil of a time keeping nannies."

"Why is that? Do you know?"

"This isn't exactly an exciting place to live, Amy. I mean, the closest movie theater is a good forty-five-minute drive. And shopping? Forget it. You've got to go into Austin or San Antonio to find a decent place to shop. And as for eating out, if you don't belong to the country club, you're pretty much limited to barbecue or Tex-Mex.''

Amy shrugged. ''Those things aren't very important to me.''

''I agree,'' Lorna said. ''Of course, I get to travel quite a bit for my job. Being a nanny six days a week really ties you down, plus it isn't easy. Are you real sure you want to do this? I mean, we did kind of pressure you.''

Amy wasn't completely sure of anything except the need to hide from Cole, but she smiled and said, ''I'm sure.''

Lorna grinned. ''This is going to be like old times.''

Amy nodded, but she knew nothing would be like old times, not for her, at least. Her life had changed irrevocably the day she married Cole Jordan, and she would spend the rest of it looking over her shoulder.

Bryce kissed his grandmother good-night, then walked over to where his mother stood talking with Claudia. She turned to him and smiled. ''Leaving?''

''Yeah, I think I'd better. The girls are getting wild, which means they're overtired.''

''So I noticed,'' his mother said dryly.

Bryce's eyes briefly met Claudia's. In hers he saw understanding and empathy. All the Hathaway siblings understood that their mother would never be the storybook, doting grandmother. Kathleen Bryce Hathaway loved her grandchildren, but she had no patience for behavior that was less than perfect.

And in Bryce's experience, no child was perfectly behaved. Children were children, not miniature adults. But there was no point in expressing the sentiment, because in this one way, his mother and his grandmother were alike. Each held strong views on the subject, and neither would ever change.

"Before you leave, dear," his mother continued, "I'd like a private word with you."

"That's my cue to disappear," Claudia said, grinning. She lifted her arms. "Gimme a hug, big brother."

Once Claudia was gone, his mother said, "Bryce, I've never known you to be impulsive—at least not since you became an adult."

Bryce instantly realized what was coming.

"So do you think it's wise to have hired Lorna's friend to supervise the girls without knowing anything about her?"

"Well, I do know she's Lorna's friend, and Lorna seems to think highly of her."

"Yes, but from what I gather, Lorna only knew her for a brief period of time many years ago. We know nothing about her people or her morals or anything else really." Kathleen frowned. "It worries me.

Don't you think you should at least check her credentials?''

''I intend to.'' Bryce had already decided he would ask Amy for her references and give them a call.

''Good. In our position it pays to be careful, you know.''

''It pays *any* parent to be careful.''

''Well, of course, but people like us have to be doubly careful.''

Bryce bit back what he really wanted to say. Instead he just kissed his mother good-night and went to round up his daughters. As they walked home, he thought about his mother's concerns. His mother had her faults—the priority she placed on position and wealth being uppermost among them—but at bottom she was a sensible woman who didn't worry needlessly. And when she did express concern, her reasoning was usually sound.

Why *had* he been so impulsive tonight? His mother was right. It wasn't like him. Normally he thought things through and investigated all aspects of a situation before he acted. Yet in the case of someone to care for his children—a job that was crucially important—he had acted on instinct, never mind the fact he had belatedly decided it might be wise to check Amy's references.

Why?

Later, as he supervised the girls in their bedtime

rituals, he still hadn't come up with an answer to his impulsive act. It was only as he climbed into bed and turned out the bedside lamp that the answer came to him, and it startled him.

Something about Amy Gordon reminded him of Michelle. Bryce punched up his pillow and turned on his side.

Amy didn't look like Michelle. Michelle had been blond with gray-blue eyes. She'd also been taller than Amy, an all around bigger woman. Yet there was something, some quality the two women shared, although Bryce couldn't exactly put his finger on it.

He thought about his impulsive act for a long while before finally deciding it didn't matter why he'd acted the way he had. For some reason he liked Amy and he instinctively trusted her. No, he didn't know a lot about her background, but he was a good judge of people, and he would lay odds Amy Gordon was a good person and her references would all check out.

So he wasn't sorry he'd offered her the job. In fact, he had a strong feeling she would be the best nanny his girls had ever had.

"So tell me about your brother," Amy said. She and Lorna were sitting on the porch—Lorna in the swing, Amy in a nearby rocking chair. Each sipped from a glass of wine. The heat of the day had finally succumbed to nightfall and the strengthening wind that promised rain before morning. It was so peaceful sitting there in the moonlight, listening to crickets chirping and the wind rustling through the leaves of the big magnolia tree that dominated the front yard. Amy could feel all the stress and worry of the past couple of days falling from her shoulders.

"Bryce is one of the good guys," Lorna said. "Of course, I *am* prejudiced since he's my brother, but even so, it's true. I admire him and respect him more than just about anyone in the world."

Amy couldn't help the stab of envy. She had always wanted brothers and sisters. "What happened to his wife?"

"Ovarian cancer. She died three years ago."

"That's tough."

"Yes, it was. We were all pretty broken up about it. Michelle, well, she was special. We all loved her. Even Mother."

The way Lorna said "even Mother" piqued Amy's curiosity, yet she hesitated to comment. She didn't want to overstep. So she was glad when Lorna continued without prompting.

"See, the thing is, my mother wanted Bryce to marry Tara Kenyon, so it really was remarkable that Michelle won her over so quickly."

"Why'd your mother want him to marry Tara?"

"Because it would enhance her position and add to the family's wealth," Lorna answered matter-of-factly. "Believe me, it had nothing to do with her thinking Tara would be a good wife to Bryce, although, to be fair, I think Tara would have been a good wife. The problem is, and always has been, that no matter how Tara feels about him, I don't believe Bryce is in love with her. I think he has a high regard for her—unlike me and Claudia, who aren't swayed by her charms." She laughed at this, then grew serious again. "He and Tara grew up together. They have a lot of interests in common, and they've always been friends, but from what I can see, that's as far as it goes for him."

"What was Michelle like?"

"The word that describes her best is *warm*. She was a warm, loving woman who rarely found fault with anyone. You just couldn't help responding to her. It's hard to dislike someone who so obviously likes you."

Amy could hear the smile in Lorna's voice. "She sounds wonderful."

"She was. Not perfect. I mean, she was human. But she *was* wonderful. In addition to being so nice, she had a great sense of humor, and a sense of fun." Lorna pushed harder on the swing, and it squeaked in protest. "Damn. I keep forgetting to oil this thing. Anyway, we had some good times together." Her voice softened. "I miss her."

Amy felt an ache of sympathy along with another twinge of envy. What must it be like to be loved so much, not just by your husband but by his family?

Amy had never known that. Oh, she'd been loved by *her* family, but Cole hadn't ever really loved her. She'd been a possession to him, something it had taken her a while to realize. And he wasn't close to his family, who lived in Michigan, so Amy had never had a chance to know them. That fact alone should have been a warning signal and should have told her something important about Cole's character, but she hadn't realized that until it was too late.

"What about the girls?" she said after a moment. "Did they have a hard time after their mother died?"

"Yes. For months they cried for her. But kids are pretty resilient, especially when they're surrounded by lots of family who love and support them. They've bounced back remarkably well, I think. I have to warn you, though. Susan is a handful. She's a big reason Bryce hasn't been able to keep the nannies he hires."

"How many nannies has he had?"

"Truthfully, I've lost count. At least six."

Amy felt a twinge of alarm. Six. "And they all left because of Susan?"

"I'd say she was the biggest factor."

Amy pictured the seven-year-old with her lively eyes and curly hair. She was cute as the dickens and obviously a high-spirited child, but she didn't seem any worse than some of the children Amy had handled in preschool. "What, exactly, did Susan do to drive them away?"

"Nothing really awful. She's just mischievous. And she's sly. When she doesn't like someone, she'll sabotage her, which is what she did to the nannies. Things like putting lizards in their jewelry box or salt in the sugar bowl or constantly hiding their glasses. That kind of thing."

"She didn't like *any* of them?"

"Not really, although a couple of them quit because they couldn't take living in Morgan Creek and having such a limiting kind of job. I mean, I told you, there's just not much to do here."

"As I said before, I'm not looking for excitement. With Calista, I wouldn't go out much anyway, even if I lived somewhere with a lot going on." Amy smiled. "Anyway, I have you, so I won't be lonely."

"I know. Isn't it great? I'm going to love having you here. I've missed having a best friend."

"But surely you've got friends here. After all, you grew up here."

"Yes, but most of my girlhood friends are gone. Some married and moved away. Others found better career opportunities in Austin or San Antonio. Oh, I've got friends. But no one I feel really close to except Claudia, and I'm afraid Claudia won't stay here, either."

"Really? Why not? Is she getting married?"

"No, nothing like that. In fact, that's a lot of the problem. There aren't many eligible young men around here. They leave, too, and go to Austin or Dallas or Houston. That's where the good jobs are.''

''But what about your family's business? Surely you employ a lot of people.''

''Yes, but mostly the jobs here are blue-collar. Not that there's anything wrong with blue-collar workers, but the guys here don't have a lot in common with my sister, even if they weren't intimidated by the idea she's a Hathaway. There are a few management jobs, but not many, and Bryce and my father and I have the three highest level positions.''

''What about sales? You've got a sales staff, don't you?''

''Of course. But they're based all over. Our Morgan Creek facility is our main plant. It's where the company began and it's still the biggest facility, but we now have twelve other smaller plants dotted around the state.''

''So is Claudia going to transfer to another location in a bigger city?''

''No. The truth is, she doesn't like working in the business.''

''What does she want to do instead?''

''Actually, she's applying for teaching jobs around the state.''

''I didn't know she was a teacher.''

''She's never taught, but she's investigated getting a teaching certificate. She has an MBA and could teach at either the high school or college level. She'd like to teach business subjects.''

By now Amy had finished her wine and was beginning to feel the effects of the wonderful dinner and the three glasses of wine she'd had over the course of the past few hours. She yawned, even though she tried not to.

''You're tired,'' Lorna said instantly. ''Of course you're tired. Where's my head? You drove all day, then I dragged you to a dinner party and now I'm keeping you awake chattering away.''

''I've enjoyed every minute of the evening,'' Amy said. ''But I *am* tired.''

Lorna got up to the tune of more squeaking. ''I've got to remember to oil this swing tomorrow.''

Amy stood, too, and together the two old friends walked into the house. Lorna closed the door behind them and turned the dead bolt.

''So you *do* lock your doors,'' Amy said. ''I wondered.''

''We never used to, but things have changed…even in Morgan Creek. Plus I'm a woman alone.''

Amy nodded. She was glad Lorna locked her doors. She was afraid she wouldn't have felt safe otherwise. She wondered if the reason was the reality of life in the present day or her fear of Cole. She guessed it was probably a combination of the two.

After saying good-night to Lorna, Amy quietly

climbed the stairs. She undressed and prepared for bed in the bathroom adjoining the bedroom she and Calista were using, then silently tiptoed across the floor and slid into bed next to Calista.

Very gently, she kissed her sleeping daughter's warm cheek. A surge of love nearly overwhelmed her as she breathed in Calista's sweet-smelling skin.

I love you so much, precious girl. I'll never let anything hurt you again.

As if Calista had heard Amy's silent vow, she sighed deeply and flung her arm across Amy.

Smiling, Amy snuggled next to her baby. Then she closed her eyes and drifted into sleep.

Chapter Four

"Why don't I call Bryce and ask him if we can pick up the girls? We'll take them and go do something fun today."

It was the next morning, and Amy and Lorna were sitting at the kitchen table over their second cup of coffee. Calista had finished eating her breakfast of waffles and strawberries and was sitting on the floor nearby playing with Bear, telling him stories that seemed to prominently feature Buttercup the cat. Right now she was saying, "And kitty likes you, Bear. She said you're nice. Do you like her?"

"What did you have in mind?" Amy asked, thinking this would give her an opportunity to get to know the girls before officially beginning her job as their nanny.

Lorna tipped her cup up and finished her coffee before answering. "I don't know. What do you think? We could go to the club and let the kids swim. We could have lunch poolside. Or we could pack a picnic lunch and drive to this park I know in San Marcos. There are swings and slides and teeter-totters. There's a little brook that runs through it, and there's even a pond with ducks. Calista would love it."

"The park sounds great." Amy loved to swim, but she didn't like the idea of being around lots of people to whom Lorna would have to introduce her. You just never knew when someone might know someone who knew Cole. Amy knew that was a long shot and she probably didn't need to worry, but she also knew she couldn't be too careful. The women who ran the underground network that had helped her with all her new documentation and references had emphasized that point over and over again.

"Trust no one," they'd said. "Always be on your guard."

"I prefer the park, too," Lorna said. "Okay, I'll call Bryce."

Five minutes later everything was settled. Lorna reported that Bryce was only too happy to let them have the girls for the day because there were several things at work and at home that needed his attention, and it would be a lot easier to do them if the girls weren't there. "An understatement, if I ever heard one," she said wryly. "I told him we'd be there by ten-thirty."

Amy looked at her watch. It was already nine-fifteen. "Do I have time for a shower?"

"Of course. Go ahead and take yours now, then I'll take mine."

"What about the picnic lunch?"

"No big deal. I've got sandwich stuff and some plums and drinks. I'll get that ready while you're showering. And we can stop and pick up some chips and cookies on the way."

An hour later, they loaded up Lorna's SUV, which had a built-in safety seat for Calista, so they didn't have to fool with taking Amy's out of her car. They pulled through the security gates of the Hathaway compound at exactly twenty-five minutes after ten.

"Right on time," Lorna said.

Amy studied Bryce's home with interest since this was where she'd be living and working starting Monday. Like the main house, it was red brick and two stories, but it was built on a much smaller scale. It was still big, though, at least as big as Lorna's. And like Lorna's, the surrounding grounds were beautiful and filled with trees. There were several large live oaks—one flanking the right side of the house, the others visible toward the back of the property, a couple of tall pines, a sweet gum and several other varieties Amy couldn't identify. Red flowering crepe myrtles dotted the front and side yards, and periwinkles, lantana and plumbago bloomed from flower beds on either side of the front door.

The girls had obviously been watching for them, because Lorna had no sooner braked to a stop in the driveway than the front door flew open and they came running out. "Aunt Lorna, Aunt Lorna!" they cried, just as if they hadn't seen her in weeks.

Amy smiled. She was looking forward to caring for these two despite what Lorna had said about Susan's behavior. Today, like Calista, they were dressed in shorts, T-shirts and sturdy sandals.

"Hi, Calista," Stella said, coming around to the passenger side of the car and peering inside.

"Should I take Calista out?" Amy asked Lorna.

"I wouldn't. I'm not planning to go inside."

A moment later Bryce appeared in the doorway. Amy's heart gave a surprising little flutter as he walked forward and their gazes met.

"Good morning," he said, smiling at her.

"Good morning." *Behave,* she told her heart sternly. *This man is going to be your employer, nothing else.*

"How was your first night in Morgan Creek? Did you sleep well?"

"I slept very well, thank you."

"I slept very well, too," Lorna said dryly.

Bryce laughed. "I wasn't ignoring you."

"Yes, you were. But that's okay. I'm used to being ignored."

"Don't pay any attention to her," he told Amy.

"See?" Lorna said, laughing. "What did I tell you?"

"Women," Bryce muttered, but he was grinning, and Amy could see he enjoyed bantering with his sister.

"Men," Lorna countered.

Turning back to Amy, Bryce said, "Last night I forgot to ask you if you could furnish me with some references."

Thank God the underground network was so thorough, Amy thought. "Yes, of course. I'll bring them with me Monday morning. Or, if you want them sooner, I could bring them over when we get back tonight."

"No, that's okay. Monday's fine."

Amy smiled. "All right."

"Now, you girls behave yourselves," he said, turning his attention to his daughters. "Listen to Aunt Lorna and Mrs. Gordon and don't give them any trouble."

"We won't," they answered in unison.

"Because I'm going to ask for a full report when you get back." He winked at Amy.

"They'll be good," Lorna said, "because if they aren't, we'll beat 'em."

"You have my permission," Bryce said.

But the girls just laughed, and Amy knew they knew their father and aunt were teasing them. She was glad to see Bryce had a sense of humor, because she would have hated working for someone who didn't.

"Have fun," he said as the girls piled into the car, one on either side of Calista, and buckled into their seat belts.

"We will," they shouted.

"We'll see you about five," Lorna said.

"Be careful driving."

Bryce stood in the driveway and watched while they drove away. As they pulled out of the compound, Amy felt happier than she'd felt in a long while. She liked Bryce Hathaway, and she liked his girls.

Maybe her luck had finally changed.

Bryce was sitting in his study and had just begun reading the July production report from the Morgan Creek plant manager when the phone on his desk rang. Picking it up, he punched the on button. "Hello?"

"Good morning!"

Bryce put the report down. "Good morning, Tara."

"The party last night was fun."

"I'm glad you enjoyed it."

"Oh, I did. Daddy did, too. He said your grand-mother is amazing and will probably outlive him."

"I wouldn't be surprised."

"She looked beautiful, didn't she?"

He smiled. "She did."

"Is she still angry with you?"

"I'm afraid so."

"You're brave to buck her."

"I don't like bucking her, but when she's being this obstinate and unfair, I don't really have a choice."

"What's happening with Claudia and her job hunt?"

"Nothing firm yet, but she's determined, so I'm sure she'll find something that suits her."

"And I guess *you're* relieved now that you've found a new nanny."

Although this was said casually, Bryce knew Tara well enough to know it wasn't an offhand observation. "Considering the amount of trouble I've had in the past, yes, I am."

"Well, of course, I'm glad for you, too, but..." She hesitated.

"But what?"

"Well, you really don't know the woman."

"Lorna knows her," he said patiently. "Has known her for years."

"Yes, but she hasn't been in touch with her for a

long time. For all we know, Amy Gordon could have just escaped from a mental hospital.''

He knew she was right, just as his mother had been right the night before. Still he was irritated. ''Oh, come on, Tara, that's ridiculous. All you have to do is talk to Amy for five minutes or watch her with her daughter to know she's sensible and wonderful with kids. Susan and Stella took to her immediately.''

''Appearances can be deceiving. Besides, I think the girls were taken with her daughter, not with her.''

''You don't like Amy, do you?''

''Now who's being ridiculous? I don't even know her. That's my point. You don't know her, either. I just think, where it comes to the girls, we need to be extra careful.''

Bryce gritted his teeth over the way she used the word *we* to suggest she had more of a stake in his life and the life of his daughters than that of a friend.

''I appreciate your concern,'' he said more formally than he'd intended, ''but Amy is going to furnish me with letters of reference.''

''Oh. That's good, then.''

''Yes. So you see there's no cause to worry.''

''Well, good,'' she said again. ''I'm sure they'll check out just fine.'' Her voice brightened. ''However, that's not why I called. I was wondering…how would you and the girls like to come over this afternoon? We just bought a new gelding I'm dying to try out, and I know the girls love to ride. And afterward, y'all can stay for dinner.''

"I'm sorry, Tara, but the girls left about an hour ago to spend the day with Lorna and Amy and her little girl. They won't be back until five or so.''

"Oh. Well, why don't *you* just come, then? We never seem to get any time alone anymore. And it's such a nice day today, not nearly as hot as it was yesterday. We could even take a picnic lunch with us.''

"Sounds very tempting, but I'm snowed under with work. That's one of the reasons I was glad when Lorna called. Having the girls gone most of the day will allow me to get caught up without feeling guilty about ignoring them.''

"Bryce, you work entirely too hard. You know what they say about all work and no play.''

"It can't be helped. We've expanded considerably this year, and that means the work load, for me, at least, has almost doubled.'' He didn't add that if his father were carrying his own weight, it would take some of the responsibility off Bryce's shoulders, which was the crux of the current problem. Jonathan Hathaway was the CEO of Hathaway Baking, Inc., but Bryce, as vice president of operations, really ran the company.

Tara sighed, the sound clearly audible over the phone line. Bryce knew she'd intended for him to hear the sigh. "Can I at least persuade you to come for a late dinner? Just the two of us?"

"I don't have anyone to stay with the girls."

"I could come there," she said softly.

What could he answer without hurting her feelings? "I was just going to pick up some hamburgers or something tonight. I figured the girls would be tired."

"I didn't mean you should *cook* for me, silly. I'll bring dinner. You won't have to worry about a thing. I'll make my famous lemon chicken and rice and bring that chocolate cake you like so much."

Why was he so reluctant? Because he felt guilty, he forced a lot more enthusiasm into his voice than he felt. "That sounds great. I'll chill some wine for us."

They hung up after agreeing that she should come at six. Bryce sat pensively for a long moment afterward, reviewing the conversation and its implications. He was going to have to do something about Tara. Coasting along like this wasn't fair to her, and it was becoming increasingly uncomfortable for him. He knew she expected their relationship to move to another level, and if it wasn't ever going to, he needed to make that clear to her in a way that wouldn't completely ruin their friendship.

And whatever he decided to do, he needed to do it soon.

* * *

Amy sighed in contentment. They'd just finished
their lunch, and she and Lorna were lying on a blanket in the shade of a big oak tree. Propped up on
their elbows, they were watching the children wade
in the shallow brook. At first Amy had been reluctant
to allow Calista to go into the water without her, but
she'd soon realized she was being overprotective.
The brook couldn't have been more than four inches
deep, and either Susan or Stella or both were holding
Calista's hand at all times. Plus they were only a
dozen feet away.

"Those girls would love to have a little sister,"
Lorna commented.

"If your brother marries Tara, maybe they will."
As soon as she said it, Amy realized that if Bryce
did get married, she'd probably be out of a job. That
was a sobering thought.

Lorna made a face. "God, you don't know how
much I hope he doesn't marry her."

"What, exactly, is it about her that you dislike so
much? I mean, you said yourself she'd probably
make him a good wife."

Lorna brushed some crumbs from the blanket.
"The main thing is she's totally self-centered. I mean
totally. She's not the least bit interested in anyone
else, especially not any other woman. She goes out
of her way to be charming with men, but she rarely
gives another woman the time of day. Oh, she pre-

tends to be interested in me and my sisters, but only because of Bryce. When he's not around she doesn't even bother to pretend.''

Amy sat up and hugged her knees. Sunlight dappled the blanket and glistened like diamonds on the water. It really was a glorious day. She smiled listening to Calista's giggles and the older girls' laughter as they splashed around in the brook.

''I've often thought,'' Lorna said, sitting up, too, ''that Tara probably secretly rejoiced when her parents divorced, because then she became the only female in her father's life. Not that she wasn't already number one with Jake. All you have to do is watch him when she's around to see he dotes on her.''

''When did her parents divorce?''

''When she was sixteen. Her mother promptly moved to Houston—which is where she was from originally—remarried within a year and has lived there ever since with her second husband. Tara stayed on the ranch with her father.''

''Do you think Bryce will marry her?''

''I honestly don't know. It's the one subject he and I don't discuss. No matter what I think, their relationship is none of my business. Now if he *asked* for my opinion, that would be different.''

''What would you say?''

''I'd tell him to run like hell.''

Amy laughed, but the conversation had cast a pall over the day. She hardly knew Bryce, but she already felt he was too good a man to end up with someone like Tara Kenyon, especially after having been married to a woman like the Michelle whom Lorna had described last night.

Or maybe I just want to make sure I have a job.

Soon after, they gathered up the girls and their stuff and walked over to the playground area, where they spent the next hour and a half. After that they loaded up the car and drove around the park to the pond where the children fed the ducks. By four-thirty all three girls were tired and had had enough sun, and it was time to head back home.

In the car, Lorna took out her cell phone. "Before we leave, I'll just give Bryce a call. Tell him we're on our way and see if he wants me to pick up some barbecue or something for dinner."

Lorna pressed in some numbers. "Bryce?" She quickly gave him an update and asked her question about dinner. "Oh, all right. Well, we'll just head straight home, then." When she disconnected, she gave Amy a look that the children couldn't see in the backseat. "He said Tara's bringing dinner over for them."

Amy didn't comment. It was interesting that Tara Kenyon was taking dinner over to Bryce's house. How had that come about? she wondered. Had he called her? Or had she called him? Maybe their relationship had progressed further than Lorna knew.

All three children fell asleep on the way home,

and Calista didn't even wake up when they reached Bryce's house and Stella and Susan wearily climbed out.

"'Bye, Miss Amy," they said. Earlier Amy had asked them to call her that rather than Mrs. Gordon.

"Goodbye, Susan. Goodbye, Stella."

"Don't get out," Lorna said. "No sense waking Calista. I'll take the girls inside and be back in a couple of minutes."

True to her word, Lorna wasn't gone long, but when she returned to the car, Bryce was right behind her. He'd changed clothes since this morning, Amy saw. Instead of the faded denim-shorts and dark-blue T-shirt he'd had on when they'd left, he now wore pleated tan dress pants and an open-necked white cotton shirt.

He walked around to Amy's side of the car, and she pushed the button to put the window down.

Leaning in, he said, "Amy, I was wondering if you could start tomorrow night instead of Monday morning? That way I could show you around and you could get settled in and I could leave for work early on Monday."

"Sure, that would be okay." Amy caught a whiff of something masculine and woodsy—his cologne or aftershave.

"Good," he said in a relieved tone. "I have an early meeting I'd've had to cancel otherwise."

"What time tomorrow would you want me?" She

wondered if he had any idea how attractive he was. *Oh, Amy, don't be ridiculous. Of course he does.*

"Why don't you just come after dinner? Say about eight. Or is that too late for your daughter? Does she go to bed earlier?"

"No, that's fine. I'll make sure she gets a nap in the afternoon."

He smiled. "Thank you. I appreciate it."

There was that little flutter again. *Honestly,* Amy scolded herself, *you'd think you'd never had an attractive man smile at you before!*

"Do you mind having to go over there tomorrow night?" Lorna asked as they pulled out of the driveway and headed toward the compound's exit.

"No. Not at all."

"I hope you like the job, Amy. I'd love to see you stay in Morgan Creek."

"I'm sure I'll like the job. But you know, the girls won't need a nanny forever."

"No, but by the time they're too old for one, maybe something else will open up around here." Lorna grinned. "Who knows? You could meet a millionaire oilman and be living in the lap of luxury."

Amy laughed. "And yesterday you were telling me how there were no men for your sister."

Lorna laughed, too.

By now they'd reached the main gate. Lorna stopped and entered the code that would open it. They were just pulling through when a white Mercedes convertible, top down, came flying down the road from the opposite direction of town.

"Tara," Lorna said.

Tara slowed and turned into the drive. She gave them a cheery wave and bright smile as she passed, then pulled through the still-open gate. Amy grimaced. If anything underscored the differences between them, it was their mode of transportation. Amy could only guess what that late-model luxury car had cost. In contrast, Amy's little Toyota was nine years old and even when new, had been an economy model. Granted, it only had about 60,000 miles on it, but by no stretch of the imagination was it the kind of car a woman like Tara Kenyon and her ilk would ever be caught dead in.

"Did you see her getup?" Lorna asked.

Amy had caught a fleeting glimpse of a red sundress that looked as if it were either strapless or held up by tiny spaghetti straps. "Yes."

"Poor Bryce."

"He's a grown man, Lorna. And not exactly stupid, I'd say."

"No, but he *is* a man."

At that, both women began to laugh.

"Anyone who didn't know us would think we hated men," Amy said when they'd sobered again.

"I know."

"I don't hate men."

"Neither do I."

On that note they fell silent. For the rest of the way home, they didn't talk. But as Lorna turned onto her street, she said, "Do you ever think about getting married again?"

"Sometimes," Amy admitted.

"Really? You're not gun-shy?"

"Well, yes, a bit, but even though my marriage was a disaster, I had a wonderful example of what marriage can be when I was growing up." She smiled, remembering how sweet her parents had been toward each other. There wasn't a day when she hadn't seen them hugging or kissing. And she could never remember a harsh word between them. "How about you?"

Lorna gave her a rueful smile. "Actually, I think about it a lot."

Later, after a light dinner of macaroni and cheese, with salad for them and applesauce for Calista, Amy gave Calista a bath, then sat on the bed until Calista fell asleep. When she went downstairs again, she found Lorna in her favorite place, sitting on the swing on the front porch. She was holding a glass of wine.

"Help yourself," she said, inclining her head toward a half-full bottle of Merlot sitting on a wicker table next to the swing. Beside it was a clean wineglass and a dish of cashew nuts.

Amy poured herself a glass, then settled herself in

the rocking chair she'd occupied the previous evening. "It's beautiful out tonight."

"Yeah, that rain we had in the middle of the night really cooled things off nicely. But it won't last. They're predicting ninety-degree temps by the middle of the week."

A few minutes later Lorna said, "I'd love to be a fly on the wall at Bryce's house tonight."

Amy smiled. She wouldn't mind seeing what was happening at Bryce's, either.

"You can be my spy from now on," Lorna said.

But somehow Amy knew she wouldn't do that, no matter how much she liked Lorna or how much she sympathized with her feelings.

It was odd, but Amy already felt loyal to Bryce, and she knew that loyalty would only become stronger once she began to work for him.

The thought was sobering.

She realized she'd have to be on her guard at all times. She couldn't allow her gratitude to him to segue past loyalty into anything else, because that would place her job and her hiding place at risk.

Something she would never do.

Chapter Five

"What do you mean, there's no trace of them? They couldn't just vanish into thin air!" Cole Jordan punctuated his angry words by slamming his fist onto his desk. Papers flew in every direction, making him even angrier. "Dammit!" he shouted, leaping up. "I gave you the make of her car and her license number. You've got her credit card numbers, her cell phone number, her bank account number, information about her father and her hometown. What else do you need? It's been three days now. What the *hell* are your people doing? Picking their noses?"

The object of Cole's wrath was Lieutenant John McGarry of the Mobile Police Department.

"We had the make and plate number of her car out within twenty minutes of your call, Cole," McGarry said mildly. "It hasn't been seen."

He seemed entirely too calm to suit Cole.

"And as for the other stuff, so far she hasn't used her credit cards or her cell phone, and like I already reported, she doesn't keep much in her bank account. At least not the one we know about. She probably set up another account under a different name."

Cole glared at him. He didn't appreciate being reminded that his ex-wife had duped him. "Did you get a bug on her father's phone yet?"

"We're working on it. They're dragging their feet in Fort Myers."

"I don't believe this," Cole fumed. "I don't *believe* it!" Where the hell *was* she? How had a stupid bitch like Amy managed to outsmart *him?* Cole wasn't used to losing, and he didn't intend to lose for long, especially to his ex-wife.

She'd been lucky, that's all. If he hadn't been in that damned meeting with the mayor and if he hadn't warned his secretary not to call him unless it was a matter of life or death and if said secretary—who'd already been fired—had been a bit smarter, Amy would never have had two hours' lead time. He'd have known almost instantly what she'd done, and he'd have caught her by now.

Where *was* she?

Was it possible she'd gone somewhere other than Florida? Cole had been so sure that's the direction she'd take. After all, second bank account or not, she couldn't have much money, not with the sweetheart divorce settlement he'd gotten. It wasn't like she could have afforded—or even known how to get— fake passports and skipped the country.

And her father didn't have that kind of money, either. The old man was living off a small pension and his social security. Cole made a mental note to make sure and check to see if he'd recently sold his house or borrowed money against it.

He also racked his brain trying to think of any friends she might have that would hide her, but the only people she knew were right here in Mobile. Truth was, Amy hadn't had many friends, and that was the way Cole liked it. When a woman started getting chummy with other women, that's when they got ideas in their heads about being independent and crap like that.

Damn. They had to get her old man's phone bugged, because no matter where she'd gone, sooner or later she'd call her father.

He swore. It was gonna take longer than he'd first thought, but in the end he'd find her. And when he did, she was going to be sorry she'd pulled this little stunt. Real sorry. He would fix it so she never saw the kid again.

Finally calmer, he gave McGarry his instructions. When the officer left, Cole picked up the phone.

It was time to call in some favors.

Lorna helped Amy pack up her belongings and carry them out to her car. After giving her the code for the security gate entrance at the Hathaway compound, she hugged Amy goodbye.

"Now, don't worry," she said, "if you need me, I'm just a phone call away." Earlier she had given Amy her cell phone number and told her not to hesitate to call 24/7 with any problems or questions.

Amy couldn't begin to tell Lorna how grateful she was. "Thank you for everything," she said, knowing it was inadequate.

"I'm thrilled you're here. You know that." Lorna kissed Calista. "I'll see you soon, sweetie." Then she waved them off.

Calista was sad about leaving Buttercup but was mollified by getting to keep Bear. She hugged the stuffed animal tightly in her arms as if she feared Lorna or her mommy might change their minds and make her leave Bear behind, after all.

"We're on our way," Amy sang as she headed for the Hathaway compound.

They arrived at Bryce's house a few minutes before eight. The sky was that soft shade of lavender that preceded nightfall, a time of day that had always seemed melancholy to Amy, maybe because it signaled the end of something rather than the beginning. For as long as she could remember, she had preferred mornings.

While she was unbuckling Calista from her car seat, Bryce, followed by Stella and Susan, came outside. The girls excitedly took Calista's hands and led her into the house while Bryce helped Amy carry in the suitcases.

"I really appreciate you coming tonight," he said.

"I was happy to." She told herself the butterflies she felt were because she was nervous about her new job and not because his eyes were so blue and his smile so sexy and appealing. *Oh, God, who am I trying to kid?* She wondered if she would have been so quick to accept this job if Bryce Hathaway had been a geek with bad breath. The image made her smile.

Inside the house Bryce suggested they go straight up to the rooms she and Calista would occupy. Amy had a fleeting impression of warmth and comfort in the rooms downstairs before she followed Bryce up the curving center staircase to the second story. Once there he turned toward the left wing and walked down a short hallway. At the end of the hallway was a door—with a lock, Amy was pleased to see—that led into a private suite of rooms.

"I unlocked the door earlier," he said, "but once you're moved in, the only person who will ever come past this door is the woman who comes in to clean twice a week. Susan and Stella are forbidden to enter your private area unless invited.''

If that was the case, Amy wondered how Susan had managed to put a lizard in the last nanny's jewelry box.

''The girls' last nanny didn't use all the rooms, but you're welcome to,'' Bryce explained once they were inside the private area.

Amy saw three doorways opening off an inner hallway. The door on the left turned out to be a large bedroom that Bryce said was the one all the former nannies had used. There was a walk-through bathroom to what Amy was sure had originally been intended as another bedroom at the end of the hallway, although this room was now furnished as a sitting room with a comfortable-looking sofa, chair and ottoman, a generous-size TV set, a bookcase and a small desk and chair. Across the hall was another large room that held a large toy box, a child-size rocking chair, a child's table and chairs, a twin bed with safety rails and a dresser.

''This furniture and the toys were stored in the attic from when the girls were little,'' Bryce said at Amy's surprised expression. ''I had them brought down earlier today.''

''That was awfully nice of you.'' Thinking about how few toys Calista had, Amy walked over to the toy box and idly opened the lid. She blinked. It was filled with toys and a stack of children's books.

"Michelle—my wife—never threw anything away," he explained. "I figured Calista might like them."

"Oh, this is wonderful," Amy said, touched by his thoughtfulness. "She'll be thrilled." Then she frowned and looked around. "Where'd the girls go?"

"Susan and Stella took Calista to their playroom in the other wing. They'll be fine," he added in response to her worried expression.

Amy nodded, but she didn't feel easy about Calista being out of her sight. She knew she had to work on this. It wasn't good for Calista for Amy to hover over her constantly. But it was hard not to feel panicky when she couldn't see her daughter, even though logically Amy knew her reaction was due to a need to keep Calista safe from Cole rather than to any other perceived danger.

"If there's anything else you want or need, all you have to do is tell me," he said. "I want you to be comfortable." Then he grinned. "I want you to stay."

Amy smiled. "Lorna told me about your nanny troubles."

"Hope she didn't scare you."

"I don't scare easily. Besides, I think your daughters are adorable."

"If Lorna warned you, she must have also told you about Susan."

"Yes, but that doesn't scare me, either. I'm used to kids acting out."

He nodded. "She tests people."

"To see what we're made of?"

"That's my theory."

"Well, I may look like I'm soft and easy, but I'm not." There was a harder edge to her voice than she'd intended. Better be careful, she thought. Better quit allowing thoughts of Cole to color what you say and do.

"Good. My girls need a firm hand. Since their mother died, they're indulged too much." For a moment, sadness shadowed his eyes, but it was quickly banished. "Do you want to see the rest of the house now or do you want to get unpacked first?"

"I can unpack later, after I get Calista to sleep."

"Okay. Follow me, then."

"First, I have something for you." Amy reached into the side pocket of her tote bag and extracted the letters of reference provided to her by the underground network. When he called, they would all check out, for the network had given her a past in Shreveport to match her new documentation. What Amy would have done if she hadn't found out about the network or if her father hadn't taken out a home equity loan to enable her to finance a new life, she didn't know. Thank God she hadn't had to find out.

Bryce took the letters. "Thanks."

Then he led the way to the other second-floor wing

which was laid out in the same pattern as her wing. The two rooms connected by the bathroom were Stella's and Susan's bedrooms, furnished in a way any little girl would cherish, with canopy beds and beautiful companion pieces—armoires and vanity tables and nightstands—plus dozens of shelves for their dolls and keepsakes. Stella's room was decorated in shades of pale pink and green, while Susan's sported bolder shades in coral and lime.

"Pretty," she commented.

"The girls chose the colors, and Lorna did the decorating," Bryce said.

The third room was a playroom, and that's where they found the girls. In addition to a TV set and a VCR/DVD player, the room contained a big table where the girls could study or play, a sturdy chintz-covered sofa, a desk holding a computer and printer, and several built-in cabinets and bookshelves loaded with books and games.

The three of them were seated on the floor, and Susan and Stella were helping Calista dress a doll. They looked up when Bryce and Amy entered.

"Mommy!" Calista held up the doll. "Lookit my doll."

"She's very pretty, but she's not really *your* doll, honey, she belongs to Susan and Stella."

Stella gave Amy one of her shy smiles. "I don't play with that doll anymore. I gave her to Calista."

Not to be outdone, Susan piped up with, "She can have my baby dolls, too. I only like Barbies now."

Amy didn't want the girls to continue giving Calista things with the idea she could keep them. She especially didn't want Calista to think all she had to do was indicate she liked something and she'd get it. Deciding she'd better set some ground rules right now, Amy said pleasantly but firmly, "It's very nice of you girls to want to share, and I know Calista will enjoy playing with your dolls while she's here, but they'll still be yours."

Calista frowned. "Mine!" She clutched the doll tighter.

"No, sweetheart, the doll is not yours. The doll belongs to Stella, but she's being very nice and allowing you to play with it for now."

Calista's lower lip protruded and she gave Amy an obstinate look from under lowered lashes.

Amy smothered a smile and said sotto voce to Bryce, "Three-year-olds can be very stubborn."

"So can seven- and eight-year-olds." He, too, was holding back a smile.

Susan looked as if she wanted to protest Amy's decision, but she didn't. Instead she studied Amy thoughtfully. Amy wondered what was going through the child's mind.

"Now we're trusting you girls to take good care of Calista," Bryce said. "Mrs. Gordon and I will be downstairs."

"Okay, Dad," Stella said.

"'Kay," Susan echoed.

"Um, I told the girls to call me Miss Amy, if that's all right?"

"Miss Amy it is, then," he said.

"What time do the girls normally go to bed?" Amy asked as she and Bryce descended the stairs.

"During the school term, I like them in bed by eight-thirty. They can read for a while, but it's lights-out at nine. In the summer I'm a lot more lenient. Usually it's ten before they settle down, sometimes later if we've gone somewhere."

Amy could see she might have to make sure Calista had a nap every day, because it would be hard to get her down at her normal time of eight o'clock if the girls were still awake. "Will it be my responsibility to get them to bed?"

"Only when I'm not here. When I'm home, I like being hands-on."

Amy liked that. Not that she would have minded bedtime duty. It was just that she thought it was important for parents to be involved in their children's lives. If Cole had been a different kind of parent, she might have stuck it out with him, even though he wasn't a great husband. In fact, it was his treatment of Calista as a possession rather than a child to love and nurture that had pushed Amy into finally leaving him.

By now they were downstairs, and Amy turned her

attention to the layout of the rooms. To the left of the front door was a large living room done in shades of browns and blues with touches of peach. It was beautifully furnished. There was a baby grand piano in one corner, and over the fireplace a large family portrait.

Amy walked over to get a closer look. It had been taken while Bryce's wife was alive and the girls looked to be about two and three.

"That was taken two years before Michelle died," Bryce said, walking up behind her.

Amy nodded. Michelle Hathaway was a lovely woman. Not beautiful, but sweet looking with an infectious smile and a face that said she was happy in her own skin. "She looks like such a nice person."

"She was. Everyone liked her." He added softly, "I miss her."

Amy glanced up at him. She liked that he wasn't afraid to express his feelings. Even though Michelle Hathaway had died young, she'd been a lucky woman to have been married to a man like Bryce.

A few minutes later they walked back to the entryway, and Bryce showed her the powder room under the stairway and the coat closet next to the powder room. On the right side of the house there was a dining room, smaller than the living room, through which you could walk into a large eat-in kitchen. Off the kitchen were a walk-in pantry and a good-size utility room. Also on the main floor—behind the living room—were two smaller rooms that opened off a secondary hallway. One was Bryce's home office, he explained, containing state-of-the-art computer equipment, and the other was a guest bedroom with an attached bath.

"This used to be the master bedroom," Bryce said, indicating the office and guest bedroom, "but I had it gutted, and we broke up the space to make these two rooms."

Amy frowned. "But where do *you* sleep?"

He laughed. "Back here." Opening a door at the end of the secondary hallway she hadn't noticed before, he said, "We built this addition the year before Michelle died. It was her pet project. Would you like to see it?"

"I'd love to."

Wow, Amy thought as he ushered her in. The master suite consisted of a large bedroom with fireplace, a separate dressing room with walk-in closets—one filled with his clothes, the other empty. Michelle's, she thought, wondering if it had been painful for him to part with her things. There was a huge bathroom, too, with a Jacuzzi tub in the middle of the room and a skylight overhead.

"Very nice," she said.

The bedroom itself was a place to relax as well as sleep. One third of the room was a sitting area with two love seats, reading lamps and a beautiful antique desk.

"Michelle enjoyed sitting there and writing out thank-you notes or letters," he said when he noticed Amy's gaze lingering on the desk, which was tucked into the space formed by a bay window that overlooked the side yard. Amy noticed a framed photo on the dresser. Even from a distance, she recognized a laughing Michelle and Bryce, arms around each other. Both were in bathing suits standing on a beach somewhere. They looked blissfully happy. Amy wondered if Tara Kenyon had ever been in this room, and if she had, what she thought of the photo.

With the tour of the house over, Bryce took Amy back into the kitchen and showed her where everything was kept. "I'll be gone by six-thirty tomorrow morning, so you'll be on your own," he explained.

"What do the girls usually eat for breakfast?"

He made a face. "They like those toaster pastries and milk. Their last two nannies got tired of fighting with them over breakfast, so we pretty much just let them have what they wanted during the week. On the weekends, when I'm here, I make sure they eat healthier."

"I don't like Calista to have too much sugar," Amy said. "Do you mind if I try to change Susan's and Stella's eating habits?"

"Mind? I'd be in your debt if you were successful."

"Good." Amy knew she might have to make changes slowly, but she could see changes needed to

be made. Bryce was right. The girls *were* indulged
too much. It wasn't good for kids to always get their
way. They needed rules and they needed to know
those rules would be enforced.

"I'll write down my office and cell phone numbers
here," Bryce said, picking up a small notepad lying
next to a portable phone on the kitchen counter. "If
you need me, just call. Don't worry about disturbing
me."

"Okay."

After that he showed her where she could find all
emergency numbers, where he kept medicines and
first-aid supplies, then he gave her a set of keys.
"This key is for the front door, this one for the back
door, and this one is for your wing."

Amy knew she would have many more questions,
but she figured they'd gone over enough tonight. It
was getting late, and she was anxious to unpack and
get settled in.

As if he'd read her mind, he said, "That's enough
for this evening. Anything else you want to know, if
it can't wait till I get home tomorrow night, just call
me. And you can always call the main house if you
have a problem. If my mother isn't there, ask to
speak to Mrs. Janny. She's the housekeeper."

"All right."

"Feel free to help yourself to anything in the
kitchen. And if there's anything you want that I don't
have, make a list. We'll get Billy—he's Mrs. Janny's

son—to get it for you. He does all my grocery shopping for me.''

Amy couldn't imagine a life where all you had to do was give someone a list and have things like grocery shopping taken care of for you. She wasn't sure if she would like it or hate it, because she'd always kind of enjoyed shopping for groceries and preparing her own meals.

''I do have one last question,'' she said. ''Who fixes dinner for you?''

He smiled. ''Don't worry, it's not part of your job description. I take care of dinner for myself. But I will need you to feed the girls unless I give you specific instructions not to. Is that all right with you?''

''Of course.''

''Good. When you go upstairs, will you tell the girls they've got thirty more minutes before it's time for bed? Tell them I've got some e-mail to take care of, then I'm coming up.''

''Okay.''

When Amy entered the playroom, she saw the girls were now playing with a doll house, and Calista was right in the thick of things. Amy delivered Bryce's message, then said, ''Calista, honey, it's time for you to say good-night to Susan and Stella and for us to go to our own room.''

''No!''

''Calista…''

"No!" Calista's expression was downright hateful as she stared at Amy.

"Can't she just stay a little while more?" Susan said.

"No, I'm sorry, she can't."

"Why not?"

Amy gave Susan a level look. "Because I'm her mother, and I said so." Then Amy calmly lifted a struggling Calista up and into her arms. "Sometimes we don't get to do what we want to do," she said, as much for Susan's and Stella's benefit as for Calista's.

Calista began to cry.

"Hush, now," Amy said. "You'll see the girls tomorrow."

"G'night, Calista," Stella said.

Susan scowled at Amy.

Yes, Amy thought as she carried a still-crying Calista to the other side of the house and into their wing. *There definitely need to be some ground rules set and some changes made.* Even so, she wasn't discouraged. In fact, she welcomed the challenge ahead of her.

She couldn't wait to begin.

Chapter Six

For the most part, Monday and Tuesday of Amy's first week on the job went smoothly. There were a couple of minor episodes with Susan, but nothing Amy couldn't handle. Calista turned out to be the biggest problem. She was still acting up, pouting and having little temper tantrums. Amy was sorely afraid the much-feared Terrible Twos, which Calista had never gone through, had now shown up as terrible threes.

Or could her daughter's misbehavior be a delayed reaction to Amy's taking her from a familiar environment into the unknown?

By Wednesday, though, Calista seemed to have

settled down a bit and she didn't protest the oatmeal Amy fixed for her and the girls' breakfast. Remarkably enough, neither did Susan, who now seemed to realize Amy meant business about healthy eating and would not be easily manipulated. Or maybe Susan was just lulling Amy into thinking she really wasn't as much of a problem as Bryce and Lorna had hinted.

No matter. All in all, Amy was feeling pretty satisfied with herself and her new job. She was humming happily as she cleaned up the kitchen and had sent the girls out back to play before the day got too hot. She could hear them laughing and squealing, and every few minutes she peered out the back door to make sure all three were in sight. Reassured to see Stella and Susan taking turns pushing Calista on one of the swings, she finished her cleanup and prepared to go out and join them. She thought she might suggest they put on their bathing suits, and she'd turn on the sprinklers for them to run around in.

It was funny that Bryce didn't have a pool. There was certainly room for one. The main house didn't have a pool, either, which surprised Amy.

Still thinking about the absence of a pool, she had just wiped down the countertops when the front doorbell rang. Now, who could that be? Bryce had told her delivery people had to ring for admittance at the gate. And Billy, the housekeeper's son at the main house, would have called to warn her someone was coming if that were the case.

When she reached the front door, she could see through the glass panels that it was Tara Kenyon standing on the doorstep.

Oh, great. Amy couldn't think of anyone except Cole she dreaded seeing more. Taking a deep breath, she told herself she could handle Tara. Trying to make her expression welcoming, she opened the door.

"Good morning." Without waiting for an invitation, Tara stepped inside.

Amy had no choice but to move aside and allow her in, even though it was the last thing in the world she wanted. "Bryce isn't here."

"Oh, I didn't come to see Bryce," Tara said breezily. "I was in the neighborhood and thought I'd just pop by and see how you're managing."

"That was very thoughtful of you." Amy decided to give the woman the benefit of the doubt. Maybe Tara really *was* trying to be helpful. Maybe Amy had misjudged her.

"Where are the girls?" Tara said.

"Out back. In fact, I was just on my way out to join them."

"Is there any coffee?" Tara headed for the kitchen, again without an invitation.

No, I didn't misjudge her. She isn't here to help. She's here to spy. "Sorry. I just cleaned out the pot and put it away." Amy decided she wasn't going to offer to make more, either.

"How about Dr. Pepper? I know Bryce always has some in the fridge." Again that fake smile. "He knows how much I like it."

Determined not to let Tara get to her, Amy replied pleasantly. "Yes, I did notice a couple of cans in the shelf on the door."

Tara opened the refrigerator and extracted a can. She popped the top and took a long swallow. As she did, her eyes made a quick inspection of the kitchen.

Amy was glad there was nothing amiss that she could report back to Bryce, for report back to him she would. Not that Amy thought Bryce had put Tara up to making this surprise visit. Or maybe he had, she thought with a twinge of disappointment. After all, Amy didn't know Bryce yet. Perhaps he didn't completely trust her, even though she knew he'd called and checked her references, because he'd told her so Monday night and he had seemed pleased by the good reports he'd gotten.

God bless the underground network, Amy thought again. She could never pay them back for what they'd done for her, no matter how much money she might someday be able to contribute to their cause.

"Bryce tells me you're doing a good job," Tara said.

Amy knew this information had been imparted so that Amy would know Bryce confided in Tara. She smiled. "I always try to give one hundred percent to my employers."

Tara leaned against the counter and drank more of her Dr. Pepper. She eyed Amy, blatantly looking her up and down. Today Tara wore spotless white capris with a green-and-white striped tank top that fit like a second skin. On her feet were green thong sandals. She looked gorgeous and sexy. Amy knew her own outfit of faded denim shorts, navy T-shirt and worn brown sandals suffered by comparison. Oh, well. She'd never be gorgeous *or* sexy.

But I do have something you want. I'm living under the same roof as Bryce Hathaway.

Amy was instantly ashamed of herself for the nasty wish to taunt Tara out loud, just the way kids taunted one another. What was it about Tara that brought out the worst in her? Amy wondered.

"Bryce worries about Susan, you know," Tara said.

"Yes, I know."

"She's a handful."

And your point is?

"She needs a mother."

Amy shrugged. What could she say? Susan probably did need a mother. At the very least, she needed a consistent, firm hand. And for as long as this position lasted, Amy intended to give her one. "The girls are fortunate they have such a loving family…and all living so close." She kept her tone matter-of-fact.

"They need someone all the time, not just occasionally." Now Tara's voice held a hint of irritation.

Amy wanted to smile. *Good grief, this woman definitely brings out the worst in me.* "I'm sure their father would agree," she said sweetly, "but he can't change what is."

Tara opened her mouth to reply, but just at that instant, there was a scream from outside. Amy dropped the dishtowel she was still holding from her earlier cleanup and ran to the back door. Calista! Amy yanked the door open and raced outside.

Relief surged through her when she saw Calista, apparently unhurt, standing there with Susan. Stella was the one on the ground with tears running down her face. When Amy reached her, she could see the child's right knee was scraped and bloody.

"What happened?"

"She fell off the swing," Susan said.

"'Cause you pushed me too high!" Stella cried.

Susan rolled her eyes. "I did not. You're such a baby."

"I'm *not* a baby. I'm older than you!"

"So?" Susan said, sounding for all the world like an adult instead of a seven-year-old. "You're still a baby."

"Susan, that's enough." Amy knelt down to look at Stella's knee. "Come inside, honey, and we'll get this cleaned up and put some ointment on it. You didn't hurt anything else, did you?"

Stella, whose tears were now stopped, shook her head. "Nuh-uh."

"She could have really hurt herself. You should have been out here supervising the girls."

Amy whipped around. She'd forgotten Tara was there. "I told you. I was on my way outside when you arrived."

Tara's green eyes glittered. "I guess you're easily distracted."

Amy gritted her teeth. She wanted to smack the other woman's face. *Go on,* she thought. *You got what you came for. Now you can go report back to Bryce that his new nanny is careless.* Taking Stella's hand, she helped her up. Then, ignoring Tara, she said to Susan, "You and Calista come, too."

"Okay."

Amy wanted to kiss the girl for not giving her an argument in front of Tara, which would only have given the woman *more* fodder for her report to Bryce.

Susan took Calista's hand and followed Amy into the house. Still ignoring Tara, Amy headed straight for the cabinet where Bryce kept his first-aid supplies. She lifted Stella up and placed her on the kitchen countertop so that she'd have easier access to her knee. She had just finished cleaning it up when Tara said she guessed she'd go.

"I'll see you girls Saturday," she said to Susan and Stella. "Your dad is bringing you out to ride."

"He *is?*" This was from Susan.

"Yes." Tara's smile was smug as her cool gaze met Amy's. "We're going to have a picnic out by the quarry. I told him to be sure and bring your bathing suits."

Amy had a decidedly unladylike and uncharacteristic urge to give Tara the finger. She was afraid if she had to spend much time around the other woman, she would turn into a first-class bitch herself.

"Walk outside with me, Susan," Tara said. "I have something in the car for you."

"Okay."

Amy wondered why Tara hadn't brought whatever it was she was going to give Susan in with her when she came in herself, then gave a mental shrug. What difference did it make? She was just glad Tara was finally leaving. But five minutes later, with Calista and Stella settled at the kitchen table with drawing paper and crayons, Susan was still outside with Tara.

Amy decided to see what they were doing. She walked to the front of the house and opened the front door. Tara and Susan, standing by the car, were deep in conversation, so much so that at first they didn't realize Amy was watching them from the open doorway. What on earth were they talking about so intently? Amy wondered. Finally Tara glanced up. When she saw Amy, she said something to Susan, and Susan turned. A moment later the child waved goodbye to Tara and walked slowly back into the house.

Amy wanted to ask what they'd been talking about, but she knew it really wasn't any of her business. So she only said, "Calista and Stella are coloring in the kitchen."

"Okay," Susan said, running off to join them.

It was only later that Amy realized Susan had come back into the house empty-handed.

Bryce was tired, and it didn't look as if he was going to get home early, after all. The product-development meeting had lasted far longer than it was supposed to, then Ed Bloom, his purchasing manager, had informed Bryce that the shipment of butter and eggs they'd expected the day before was going to be delayed another two days because of a walkout at Clarkson Farm and Dairy, their main supplier in this part of Texas. Now Ed was worried they wouldn't be able to meet all their orders on time. And to top off the day, Lorna had passed on the worrisome news that their profit margin for the quarter would probably be down.

"I won't know until closer to the end of September, but it's not looking great right now."

Sometimes Bryce wished he could chuck it all. Just tell his father he was tired of having the lion's share of responsibility for his family's fortunes resting on his shoulders, and he was going to turn the whole mess over to him. But that feeling never lasted long. It was usually just the result of a frustrating day, and when Bryce was able to look at everything objectively again, he wondered who he was kidding. He'd never leave the company. Hell, this company was in his blood.

"Hey, Bryce, glad I caught you still here."

Bryce looked up to see Anita Farrow, the most innovative of the baking specialists he employed to develop new products, standing in his doorway. "Hey, Anita. What's up?"

"You know that vanilla I ordered from Mexico? It's great. I experimented with it for the new mini cinnamon rolls, and they taste terrific. I brought you one."

"Trying to spoil my dinner, are you?" But he took the proffered roll and bit into it. It was still warm, and the combination of butter, sugar, cinnamon, pecans and vanilla in the pastry assaulted his taste buds.

"Like it?"

"It's fantastic." Hathaway used only the best ingredients in their breads and pastries. Their products cost more than some other companies, but their customers knew they were getting the highest quality products when they bought from Hathaway. They were particularly renowned for their cinnamon rolls. "Is the vanilla the only difference between this roll and the ones we've been selling?"

"Yes."

"Well, it's a winner."

Anita grinned and gave him a high-five. Once Bryce was alone again, he picked up the phone. He'd better call Amy and tell her he was going to be late again. He hated doing it because this was the third day in a row he'd gotten stuck at the office and hadn't made it home until nearly eight. He'd been tired and hungry and not looking forward to another night of scrambled eggs for dinner. But both nights Amy had surprised him. She'd made enough dinner that there was some left for him. All he'd had to do was nuke it and eat.

Good dinners, too. On Monday she'd made a meat loaf with mashed potatoes and fresh green beans, the kind of thing Michelle had liked to cook for him. And yesterday she'd made some kind of chicken with a mushroom sauce that she'd served over rice.

She'd even managed to coerce the girls into eating both offerings. In fact, in the three days since she'd come to work for him, she'd pretty much eliminated most sweets from their diet except for Hathaway cinnamon rolls, which they were allowed to have after lunch.

He smiled. She was amazing. A godsend, no matter what Tara thought. Reminded of the phone call he'd gotten this morning, he grimaced. He'd been right when he'd accused Tara of not liking Amy. She could deny it, but Bryce knew it was true. This morning he'd told her as much.

"You're looking for things to hate about her," he'd said.

"Now why would I do that?" she'd answered.

"I don't know." He'd briefly considered the idea that Tara might be jealous of Amy, then dismissed it. Why would she be jealous? Amy was an employee of his, nothing more.

"Bryce, I'm just concerned about the girls' welfare."

"And I appreciate that, but from what you describe of this morning's event, I don't think the girls are in any danger. Hell, accidents happen. And you said yourself Stella seemed fine when you left."

He could tell Tara had wanted to continue the conversation; however, he'd told her he was late for a meeting, which was true, and they'd hung up—but not before she'd reminded him of his promise to bring the girls out to the ranch on Saturday.

He'd completely forgotten that to placate her for not being able to take them out to ride the previous weekend, he'd said they'd come this weekend. "Tara, I'm sorry, but when I said we'd come this Saturday I had forgotten about Cameron's birthday party. The girls and I are going to Austin for the day."

Remembering how disappointed and upset she was, Bryce sighed. He seemed to be breaking promises right and left. And here he was, now about to break another one, for the last thing he'd said to Amy this morning was that he would not be late tonight.

He hit the speed-dial code for home. It rang twice, then Amy answered. "Hathaway residence."

"Hi, Amy."

"Oh, hello, Bryce."

"Listen, I'm sorry, but I'm going to be late again."

"That's okay. I don't mind."

"But I don't want you fixing dinner for me again. I'll pick up a pizza on my way home."

"You don't have to do that. This morning I made spaghetti sauce and meatballs. There's going to be plenty for everyone."

"What are you? A mind reader?" he said with a laugh.

"Look, I know you said that's not part of my job description to feed you, but the truth is, I like to cook, and I have to feed myself and the girls, anyway. So why not just make more of whatever it is I'm making and feed everyone? It's no big deal."

Bryce could feel his shoulder muscles relaxing. Still he felt he should at least put up a show of resistance. "I don't like taking advantage of you."

"You're not."

"We'll make some new arrangements as far as salary goes, then."

"Bryce, you're paying me a lot already. I couldn't look myself in the mirror if I took any more."

They talked a few more minutes, then just as Bryce was going to say goodbye, Amy said, "Tara Kenyon stopped by this morning."

"Yes, I know."

"I *thought* she'd call you. She told you what happened, didn't she?"

"You mean about Stella falling off the swing?"

"Yes."

"Look, it's no big deal. The girls have had accidents before, and they'll have them again."

"I don't want you to think I'm careless or that they'll be unsupervised. It was just that I was on my way out—"

"Amy, you don't have to explain."

"But Tara made it clear that—"

"Tara tends to overreact."

For a long moment there was silence at the other end of the line. When she did speak, her voice had softened. "Thank you, Bryce. I appreciate your confidence in me."

Bryce thought about their conversation off and on for the next couple of hours and was still thinking about it as he finally got away from the office and was on his way home.

It was time to make a couple of things clear with Tara.

Amy put a covered plate of spaghetti and meatballs inside the microwave for Bryce to heat when he got home. Then she cleaned up the kitchen while the girls watched a Disney video in the older girls' playroom.

At seven-thirty Amy went upstairs to collect Calista and give her a bath. But she put up a fuss—the video wasn't over—and Amy gave in and said she could continue watching with Susan and Stella.

"I'm going downstairs to get a book to read. I'll be back," she said.

The girls barely acknowledged her remark, they were so engrossed in the story. Amy headed for the bookshelves in the living room and had just chosen a book when the phone rang. "I'll get it!" she called upstairs. Susan had an irritating habit of racing for the phone and talking to whoever called, even if the call was for Amy, and Amy was trying to break her of it.

Sure enough, when Amy picked up the portable phone and clicked it on, Susan was already talking to the caller. It took Amy a moment to realize the voice on the other end belonged to Tara.

"Is someone else there?" Tara said.

"Sorry. I didn't know Susan had answered," Amy said. "Did you want to speak to me?"

"No. I called to speak with Susan."

"Oh. All right. I'll hang up, then."

Amy disconnected, then stood there just looking at the phone. She didn't know why she was disturbed. Tara had a perfect right to call Bryce or the girls or anyone else she wanted to call. And yet Amy couldn't banish the niggling feeling of alarm. On one level she knew it was ridiculous to feel threatened by a simple phone call. On another level, she was afraid anything connected to Tara Kenyon was bad news.

She was still standing there when she heard the garage door opening. Putting the phone down, Amy walked out to the kitchen. A few minutes later Bryce entered through the back door. He looked tired, Amy thought, and no wonder. It was after eight and he'd left the house before seven this morning.

"Hi."

He smiled wearily. "Hi."

"You look exhausted."

"I am. Girls upstairs?"

"Yes. I was just heading back up to get Calista ready for bed. Your dinner's in the microwave."

He smiled his thanks. "Okay."

The video was just running the closing credits when Amy entered the playroom. "Okay, Calista," she said. "Time for your bath."

The mutinous frown Amy was beginning to dread appeared almost instantly.

"No!" Calista said, glaring at Amy.

"Yes." Amy reached down to pick Calista up.

Calista squirmed out of her grasp. "No! I don't want a bath!"

"That's too bad, because you need one, and you're going to have one."

This time when Amy reached for her, Calista kicked out at her. "That's it," Amy said. "You're going into time out." Scooping Calista up firmly, Amy marched her out of the playroom and across the hall to their wing. Taking her into her own bedroom, Amy deposited Calista in the corner beside her bed. By now Calista was wailing as if Amy had beaten her. "When you can control yourself and tell Mommy you're sorry, you can come out."

Although it hurt Amy to see her daughter so unhappy, she knew she had to be firm. Tantrums weren't acceptable. Calista had to learn that.

When Amy turned around to go into the bathroom to run the water for Calista's bath, she saw Susan standing in the doorway.

"Yes, Susan? Did you want something?"

Susan glared at her. "Tara said you were mean, and you *are!*"

There were several retaliatory things Amy wanted to say in return, but she swallowed them all. Reminding herself Susan was only seven and that the words that had come out of her mouth had been planted there by someone else entirely, she answered quietly. "I'm sorry you feel that way, Susan, but Calista has to learn she can't always have her way."

"Susan! Where are you?"

Susan gave Amy one more angry look, then yelled, "I'm coming, Daddy!" and ran off.

Once she was gone, Amy finally allowed herself to give inner vent to the fury generated by the knowledge that Tara Kenyon had discussed her with Susan, a mere child. What was the woman *thinking* to do such a thing? Did she really view Amy as that much of a threat that she would resort to this kind of low tactic to discredit her? And what should Amy do about it? Should she tell Bryce? Should she confront Tara? Or should she try to talk to Susan?

"Mommy? I sorry."

At the sound of Calista's mournful voice, Amy forced herself to put thoughts of Tara on hold. Right now Calista needed her full attention. Kneeling, she hugged her daughter, who had walked up behind her, relishing the warm sweetness of her body. "Thank you, sweetheart. I'm sorry, too. Mommy doesn't like to be cross with you."

In answer, Calista only hugged Amy harder. "I love you, Mommy."

"I love you, too, angel."

Later, as Amy sat on the edge of the tub and watched Calista happily splashing, she finally allowed herself to think about Tara Kenyon again. Although she hadn't decided just what to do, she knew she would do whatever it took to keep Calista safe here in Morgan Creek.

And if that meant she had to fight Tara Kenyon, then fight her she would.

Chapter Seven

Cole drove down the Fort Myers street slowly. It had been at least six years since he'd been to the old man's house, and he didn't want to miss it then have to turn around and come back. He looked with distaste at the houses he passed. They all looked alike to him, small and ugly. Hell, you could tell just by looking at the cars parked in the driveways or on the street that the people who lived here were struggling to look middle class, at best.

Coming from a place like this, you'd think Amy would have been more grateful for what Cole had given her. Instead she'd acted high and mighty from the start. Little bitch. Well, she'd soon get hers.

There it was.

Number eighty-six. Her father's house.

Cole pulled up in front of the stucco bungalow. He hoped Leo Summers was home. He hadn't wanted to call first. In his years as a prosecutor, Cole had learned the value of surprise. When people were taken off guard, they tended to reveal things they wouldn't let slip if they'd had any warning.

After cutting the ignition, Cole pocketed the keys and climbed out of the rented Lincoln. A minute later he stood on the stoop of his former father-in-law's home and rang the doorbell. He heard it chime, then leaned forward to peer through the small window, but Cole couldn't see anything. He almost rang the doorbell again when he saw the old man approaching.

Amy's father only opened the door as far as the safety chain would allow. His dark eyes—a bit clouded now—peered out suspiciously.

"Hello, Leo," Cole said smoothly. How old *was* Amy's father now? Seventy-eight? Eighty? Cole couldn't remember.

"Hello, Cole." Leo Summers's voice was surprisingly strong. He didn't smile.

"You don't seem surprised to see me."

"Nothing you do would surprise me."

Deciding to ignore the older man's taunt, Cole still spoke pleasantly. "Did Amy tell you I'd probably be coming?"

"I haven't spoken to Amy recently."

"When *was* the last time you spoke to her?"

"I don't remember."

"Come on, aren't you curious about why I'm here?"

"Nope."

Cole decided he was through pussyfooting around with the old man. Time to get tough. "Look, Leo, I know there's no love lost between us, but your daughter has done something illegal. Something that's landed her in big trouble. If you don't want to see her go to jail, you'll let me in, and we'll talk like civilized adults."

"I don't know what you're talking about."

"I think you do. In fact, I think you helped her." Cole couldn't believe how defiant the old man was. He didn't sound the least bit afraid. "Which means you're an accessory to a crime. Which is punishable by law." This was a bluff, but Cole figured the old man wouldn't know that.

Leo laughed. "You don't scare me, Cole. But my legs aren't what they used to be, and I'm gettin' tired of standing. Knowing you, you're not going to leave until you finally get it through your thick head that you made this trip for nothing, so I might as well be comfortable until that happens." So saying, he slid the chain off the hook and held the door open.

Now that Cole could really see Amy's father, he realized the old man hadn't changed much in six years. He was moving slower, maybe, but he still held himself with the military bearing he'd learned from his stint in the Army when he was in his twenties. Cole followed him through an archway into the small living room where it was apparent what Leo had been doing when Cole arrived, for an open newspaper was lying on a table next to a half-filled glass of water and a pair of reading glasses. Leo waved toward the couch.

"Have a seat. You want some coffee? Or a beer? I've got some Heineken in the refrigerator."

"You still drink that stuff, huh?"

"One a day," the old man said.

"Sure. I'll have a beer."

Leo disappeared into the kitchen, and Cole stood up to study the framed photos on the mantel. There was one of Amy's mother, one from Amy's college graduation, one of the kid and Amy together that looked as if it had been taken when the kid was about six months old, and one of the kid alone. That one had been taken recently, Cole saw. And from the background, Cole could tell it was taken in his backyard.

When Leo returned with his beer, Cole sat down and waited until Leo had seated himself in the chair that was obviously his favorite.

"Let's make this easy on both of us," Cole said. "Why don't you just give Amy a call and tell her to come home? If she comes now, I won't press charges against her.''

Leo picked up his water glass and slowly drank some. He set it down carefully before replying. ''You know, Cole, I never liked you. I tried to talk Amy out of marrying you, because I always knew you wouldn't be good to her. So if you think I'll help you find her if she's finally managed to get away from you, you've got another thing coming. There's nothing you can offer me and no threat you can make that'll induce me to help you. Even if I *knew* where she was. And I don't. In fact, I didn't even know she was gone.''

''Don't give me that crap, Leo! You knew what she was planning all along. Why else did you take out a loan against this house?'' Seeing the expression on Leo's face, Cole gave him a tight smile. ''Thought I didn't know that, huh? I know everything. I know that Amy hooked up with some kind of underground outfit that helps women steal kids from their husbands. And I know you financed the whole thing. Now, you tell me where she is, or I promise you, Leo, you'll be sorry. Because I'm going to find Amy no matter how long it takes, and when I do, she's going to spend the next ten or fifteen years of her life behind bars. And she'll never see Calista again.''

''What makes you think she got help from an underground organization?''

The question was asked calmly, but Cole's eyes were sharp, and he was used to studying witnesses for anything that might give away nervousness or the fact they were lying, so he saw the tremor in the old man's hands as he once more reached for his water glass. Leo was shook up by what Cole had revealed.

"All I had to do was look at her phone bills and check the numbers she called in the last month." Actually, it hadn't been *that* easy finding out who that one unidentified number belonged to, but Cole had his sources. "But that's beside the point. The point is, I know you helped her run off with Calista. And if you haven't talked to her yet, I know you will. And when you do, I want you to give her a message from me. You tell her I won't stop looking until I find her and Calista. So if she wants to save herself a bushel of trouble, she'll come back now."

School started the third week of August, and Amy was glad. Susan and Stella had been antsy the past week, probably as tired of summer as everyone else.

The first morning, Bryce went into the office late so that he could drive them to school. From now on, Billy would take them and pick them up, but Bryce said he liked doing it on the first day.

Calista cried when they left. Amy felt bad for her. Calista would be lonely with them gone most of the day, but in some ways, it might be better for her. She was growing too dependent on them to entertain her and play with her, and Amy felt she needed to learn to entertain herself.

Amy still hadn't decided what to do about the Tara problem. She'd been thinking about the woman and her dirty tricks ever since the night Susan had revealed the fact she and Tara had discussed Amy. She guessed she would have figured out something if Tara had made any other moves in her direction, but since that day she'd popped in unannounced, Amy hadn't seen her, and as far as she could tell, she hadn't called Susan again, either.

Right now, though, Amy had a more pressing problem. Today was her father's eightieth birthday, and Amy wanted, more than anything in the world, to call him. Yet she knew she couldn't. How could she? There was no doubt in her mind that Cole would either have her father's phone calls monitored— could he do such a thing in another state?—or would have access to her father's phone bills. All Cole would have to do was see a Texas number, especially on her dad's birthday, and he would know where Amy was.

All Amy could do was call her contact at the underground network and ask the woman to get in touch with her father.

Amy's eyes filled with tears as she pictured him spending his birthday alone. "Daddy," she whispered. "I am so sorry." She hadn't even been able to call and tell him when she left Mobile. She hadn't dared stop long enough, and by the time she and Calista had stopped that first night, she was afraid to reveal where they were, because then Cole would know what direction she'd gone.

Besides Calista, Amy loved her father more than anyone in the world. Damn Cole! He had taken so much away from her. Her self-respect. Her freedom. Her child. And now he'd taken her father, too.

Well, she wasn't going to let him. Maybe she couldn't call her father directly, but she *could* get word to him. Filled with energy now that she'd thought of something positive she could do, Amy gathered up Calista and headed out to her car.

"We go to the store?" Calista asked once they were on their way.

"Yes, we're going to the store. We're going lots of places. But first Mommy has to make a phone call, okay?"

"Okay." Calista was happy because Amy had allowed her to take Bear along.

Amy drove straight to the service station where she'd phoned Lorna the first day she'd arrived in Morgan Creek. She parked and, Calista in tow, headed for the pay phone. She put in her quarter and got the operator, telling her she wanted to place a collect call, then gave her the familiar number of the underground network.

"WHW. May I help you?" WHW stood for Women Helping Women.

"Will you accept a collect call from Amy Cole?" the operator asked. Amy Cole was the code name given Amy.

It only took a minute for the woman who'd answered the phone to look up Amy's name and okay the call. When the operator left them, Amy asked to speak to Regina, who was her main contact. A few seconds later, Regina's familiar southern drawl was on the line.

Amy quickly filled her in on where she was and how she could be contacted, realizing as she did so that this was something she should have done much sooner. What if something happened to her father? There was no way she'd ever know, if no one knew where she was. "I want you to get word to my father that I'm okay."

"All right."

"His phone may be tapped, though. My ex has lots of connections."

"Don't worry. We know how to relay information without giving anything concrete away. You can also send letters here. We'll repackage them and send them for you."

"What if his mail's intercepted?"

"Anything's possible, of course, but your ex is a lawyer, Amy. He knows the penalty for tampering with the U.S. mail."

"Nothing stops Cole when he wants something."

"If you're worried about that, we could have something delivered by UPS or Federal Express."

That sounded safer to Amy. She just didn't trust Cole not to plant a spy in the post office. She felt he was capable of anything. "Do I have any money left on account?"

"Don't worry about it. This is the kind of thing we're here for."

"I know, but you need your money to help women who don't have any financial resources. I do. I'm getting paid a good salary. I'll send a check along for you when I send the package for my father."

"Don't say anything in what you write to him about where you are," Regina warned.

"I know. It's better to be careful."

"Yes. And, Amy, be sure and tell your father he can write you back, care of us. Tell him to address the letter to me at our post office box address. I'll forward it to you. Unless you think that'll cause questions where you are?"

"If it does, I'll tell them you're an old friend from Louisiana who moved to Mobile."

When they hung up, Amy felt as if a load had been lifted from her shoulders. She could write her father, and he could write her. God bless the network. She would make sure she sent them a generous check.

Bryce couldn't concentrate. He'd been trying to compose a letter to the stockholders for over an hour, and he was getting nowhere. Getting up, he walked around his office. Trouble was, he had something other than the stockholders' report on his mind. Realizing he would get nowhere attempting to work, he walked back to his desk and picked up the phone, then punched in Lorna's extension. "Have you got a few minutes?"

"Sure. I'm on my way."

Good as her word, barely sixty seconds had gone by before she breezed into his office and plopped down in one of the two leather chairs flanking his desk. "Okay, what's up?"

Bryce got up and shut the outside door to his office.

"Uh-oh. This is serious," Lorna said.

"What I want to talk to you about has nothing to do with work."

"Oh?"

He sighed heavily and came around to take the leather chair opposite her. "I need some advice."

"Okay."

"It's about Amy."

"Okay," she said again, but this time she seemed wary.

"Yesterday Susan said something disturbing." When Lorna didn't say anything, just kept her steady gaze on his, Bryce continued. "She told me Tara told her Amy wasn't going to stay. Anyway, I wondered...has Amy said anything to you about leaving?''

''No! And I can't believe she is. She loves it here, Bryce. She's told me so. In fact, last night at dinner she told me she's happier here than she's been in a long time. And Calista loves it, too.''

He nodded. ''That's what I thought. So why would Tara say something like that? To Susan, especially?''

''Do you really want to know what I think?''

''I wouldn't ask you if I didn't.''

''Well, first of all, Susan's been on my mind a lot lately. In fact, Amy and I talked about her last night, and we've come to the conclusion that the reason Susan tries to drive off her nannies is because she doesn't want to get too close to any mother-like figure. If she does, that person will just leave her the way her own mother did.''

Bryce stared at Lorna.

She shrugged. ''I know. You probably think it sounds far-fetched, but Amy thinks this could be the underlying cause behind Susan's behavior. Amy's had a lot of experience with kids, and when she told me her theory, it just felt right to me.''

Bryce had always been bothered by Susan's pranks and her sometimes outright hostility toward the nannies. She'd never acted that way toward anyone else. If Amy's theory was right, it put a whole new slant on the problem.

''What I *didn't* discuss with Amy,'' Lorna went

on, "is the fact I think Susan and Stella could both care for her a great deal. Actually, I think they are already beginning to, and I think Tara senses this. I think she's viewed Amy as a threat from the very first day she set eyes on her."

"Why?"

"Oh, come on, Bryce. You know why. Amy is a doll. She's pretty and fun and smart and nice. She's got a personality that's a lot like Michelle's. Tara saw that from the get-go. When you offered Amy the nanny position, Tara immediately became alarmed. She's afraid you'll fall for Amy, and then Tara's hope of being the next Mrs. Bryce Hathaway will go right down the tubes."

Bryce stared at Lorna.

"So I think Tara is trying to reinforce Susan's subconscious fears. If she can make her believe Amy's going to leave her the way Michelle left her, then Susan won't allow herself to like Amy. In fact, she'll do her best to sabotage Amy every step of the way."

Bryce nodded slowly. Everything Lorna said made sense to him. "Any ideas about what I should do?" he finally asked.

"Yes, but first, can I ask you a question?"

"Sure."

"What are your feelings for Tara? Are you considering marrying her?"

"I've thought about it." Bryce saw the fleeting expression of disappointment that crossed Lorna's face, one she quickly disguised. "You don't like Tara, do you?"

"No. I never have."

"Why not?"

"Truth?"

"Truth."

"For one thing, she's too high maintenance. With Tara, it's always me, me, me. I don't think she ever does anything unless she feels there's something in it for her. I want better for you. And after being married to Michelle, I would think you'd want better for you, too."

On some level, Bryce recognized the truth of what Lorna had said, yet he felt her assessment of Tara was too harsh. "I said I'd thought about it," he said. "But in the past month I've realized it wouldn't work out. She and I have a lot in common, and I consider her a friend, but I'm not in love with her."

Lorna expelled a sigh. "Thank God. I was really worried about that. I mean, I would have supported you all the way if you loved her, and I'd've done my darnedest to be a good sister-in-law to her, but I wouldn't have been happy about it." She reached over and covered his hand with hers. "I love you, Bryce. I want you to be happy. And I think you've made the right decision."

"Yeah, but now what?"

"You've got to make the situation clear to Tara. And you'll need to be careful when you do it. You can't act as if you think she expects a proposal or anything. You have to let her know how you feel and don't feel, in a way that will save her pride.''

Easier said than done, he thought. ''Any suggestions?''

''Actually, I do have one,'' she said after a moment. ''You could tell her what Susan told you and ask her why she said such a thing. The conversation is bound to lead to a point where you can let her know your feelings.''

''You think, huh?''

''It's worth a try.'' She grimaced. ''I don't envy you. This won't be easy.''

An understatement if he'd ever heard one. For the rest of the day, his conversation with Lorna kept replaying in his mind. He felt her and Amy's theory about Susan was more than likely on target, which meant he needed to spend some time talking to her. Who knew? Maybe even get her some therapy, something he'd seriously considered after Michelle died. In fact, he'd wanted both girls to have some grief counseling, but his mother had been so adamantly opposed, he'd finally dropped the idea. ''Hathaways do not expose their problems to strangers,'' she'd said. ''The girls will be fine.'' He shouldn't have listened, he realized now.

He also kept thinking about what Lorna had said about Amy. Although at first he denied it to himself, Lorna was probably right about that, too. Amy was every bit as appealing as Lorna had painted her, and he *was* attracted to her. The attraction had been almost immediate, and it had only gotten stronger as he'd begun to know her better. What he would do about it, if anything, was another story, and right now, he couldn't think about that. First things first.

That meant dealing with Tara.

He picked up the phone.

Tara answered on the second ring. "Bryce! This is a nice surprise."

"Hi, Tara. I was just wondering if you had any plans for tomorrow night. I thought I might come over. There's something I wanted to talk to you about."

"Your timing is perfect," she said happily. "Daddy left today for Vegas. He's playing in a poker tournament out there this weekend, so we'll have the place to ourselves tomorrow. Come for dinner. We'll grill some tenderloin steaks. And I'll fix some mushrooms and salad to go with them."

Although Bryce didn't want to come for dinner, he didn't know how to refuse. "Sounds good. I'll bring wine."

He felt like a jerk when they'd hung up. He knew she had no idea what was coming and only hoped both he and Lorna were wrong about her expectations. But down deep he knew they weren't.

He wasn't looking forward to tomorrow night.

Chapter Eight

"The steaks were wonderful, weren't they?"

Bryce smiled. "Everything tasted wonderful, Tara. You're a good cook."

"I have many talents," she drawled.

"I never doubted it for a minute." His heart smote him at the light in her eyes, because he knew tonight would turn out far different than her expectations. He knew she was self-centered and spoiled, but he also knew she had many good qualities that Lorna had failed to see. Bryce didn't like hurting people, whether they deserved it or not, but with the present situation, it couldn't be helped.

Tara laid down her fork. "Shall I put on some

coffee to have with our dessert? I made butterscotch pie.''

Bryce felt another twinge of guilt. Butterscotch pie was his favorite, and Tara knew it. In fact, she'd asked his mother for the recipe, which had been *her* mother's and had learned to make it the way he liked it best.

''Or would you like another glass of wine and we can have our dessert later?''

''I've had enough wine, I think. Sure. Put on the coffee.''

When she got up, he got up with her and started stacking their plates to carry into the kitchen.

''You don't have to do that, Bryce. You go and relax in the living room. Concetta will clean up in the morning.''

Bryce liked Concetta, the Kenyons' longtime housekeeper, and hated making more work for her, but it wasn't his house or his business, so he put the plates down again and went into the living room. He made himself comfortable in one of the big leather chairs that sat on either side of the fireplace. Molly, the Brittany spaniel that had once been Jake's number-one hunting companion but was now too old for sport, sank down by his feet. Bryce bent down to scratch her silky head.

Bryce loved dogs, but Stella was allergic to their dander, just as Michelle had been.

Just then Tara walked in carrying a laden tray. She

looked at him quizzically. "Why don't you come over here and sit?" Putting the tray down on the coffee table, she sat on the couch. Her green dress, the exact shade of her eyes, rode up to expose a length of shapely thigh.

Bryce had purposely avoided sitting on the couch, figuring it would be easier to say what needed saying if they had some distance between them, but he had little choice now but to comply with her request.

The next few minutes were spent drinking their coffee and eating their pie.

Finally Bryce knew he could put off his mission no longer. He set his empty coffee cup down, declined her offer of more, and said, "Tara, there's something we need to talk about."

There was no mistaking the eagerness that lit her green eyes.

Damn. Bryce would have given anything to be somewhere else. Anywhere else. "Susan told me something that greatly disturbed me."

The smile on her face turned into a perplexed frown. "Oh?"

"She said you told her Amy wouldn't stay on as their nanny."

For a moment Tara looked like a kid caught raiding the cookie jar, but she quickly recovered. "So? She *won't* stay forever." Although he was sure she hadn't meant to reveal it, there was a defensive note in her voice. "After all, the girls will soon be too big for a nanny."

"Did you explain that's what you meant when you talked to Susan? Because that's not the way she took it."

Irritation flashed in her green eyes, and this time she made no effort to disguise it. "I don't remember exactly what I said. What's the big deal? Is this important, Bryce?"

"Yes, I think it is."

"Why? I mean, Amy is just a nanny. Anyway, Susan doesn't like her. I was trying to reassure her by what I said."

"Amy's the best nanny we've ever had, and I think, given a fair chance, she can win over both girls. But if you keep undermining her, she won't have a fair chance."

"I'm more than a little upset by your attitude, Bryce." But now there was fear mixed in with the defiance in her voice.

"I'm sorry, Tara, I don't mean to hurt your feelings, but I want you to refrain from talking about Amy with the girls. I've been assured she's not considering leaving, and I want the girls to know that. The thing is—" He held up a warning hand to stave off the rejoinder she'd opened her mouth to make. "Let me finish, okay? What I'm trying to emphasize here is that we feel Susan purposely tries to run off the nannies because she's subconsciously afraid if she gets too close to them, she'll just get hurt when they *do* leave, the way she did when her mother died.''

''*We?* Since when are you into psychological analysis? I'll bet this is your new nanny's theory, isn't it?''

Ignoring the sarcasm in her voice, he answered evenly. ''Yes, Amy's the one who suggested this was the reason behind Susan's behavior. But as soon as I heard what she thought, I felt it was accurate.''

''Oh, for heaven's sake, Bryce. You don't really believe that psychobabble, do you? Didn't you consider that your new nanny is being a bit self-serving here? I mean, it's a lot better for you to think Susan is afraid Amy will desert her than it is for you to realize Susan might just see through her for what she is.''

''What do you mean, what she is?''

''A woman looking out for her own best interests. A woman who sees what a cushy job she has, working for a man who's wealthy and eligible and vulnerable.''

''Amy's not like that.''

''How do you know what she's really like? How do any of us?''

''We're not discussing Amy. We're discussing what you did and what you said. Susan also told me you told her Amy was mean.''

''That's not true. She's the one who said Amy was

mean, and I only questioned her as to why she thought so.''

''I see. And you didn't think to talk to me about this?''

''You know, Bryce, I'm really upset by your attitude. We've known each other our entire lives. I thought you'd want me to develop a relationship with the girls and to encourage them to confide in me. If I come running to you every time they tell me something in confidence, how can we build any kind of trust between us?''

''Tara...'' He sighed. This was not going well. ''Of course I don't want you tattling to me every time the girls tell you something in confidence, but this is different.''

''How is it different?''

''It concerns their welfare.''

''And I don't have their welfare at heart? Is that what you're saying?'' There were two bright spots of color on her cheeks.

''You're twisting every word out of my mouth. I just don't want the girls pulled in two different directions. Right now it's important that all the adults in their lives work toward the same goal. And that means supporting Amy.''

''I don't understand why you're taking *her* side against *me*.''

''Tara, it's not a matter of sides. It's a matter of Susan's and Stella's well-being. I just happen to think Amy is the best thing to happen to them in a long time, and I don't want to see her run off if I can possibly prevent it.''

''It's obvious she's got you fooled, but I'm warning you, Bryce, she's not what she seems to be.''

''What do you mean?''

''I mean just that. There's something strange about her. Something not quite right.''

''You're imagining things, Tara. You just don't like her, so you're seeing what you want to see, not what is.''

''I know that I saw her using the pay phone at Lowell's Service Station on Monday. What reason could she have for using a pay phone when there's a perfectly good phone at your house?''

''Maybe because she was out and had to make a call right then?''

''Why doesn't she ever get any mail? Or phone calls?''

''How do you know she doesn't?''

''Susan told me.''

''Susan *told* you? She just volunteered that information?''

When Tara didn't answer, Bryce said, ''You asked her, didn't you? You were pumping her for information.''

''*Pumping* her! Yes, I *did* ask her. You may be blind about your new nanny, but I'm not.''

''Don't question Susan about Amy again, Tara.''

Bryce's tone had hardened. He didn't want to hurt her, but he also didn't intend to put up with any more interference from her, either.

"Just what are you trying to say to me, Bryce?"

"I think I've made myself perfectly clear. I don't want you putting ideas in Susan's or Stella's heads. It's my job to supervise their relationship with Amy, not yours."

At this, she jumped up. She was furious, and she no longer cared if he knew it. "I can't believe you're taking her side against me."

Bryce stood, too. "Tara, be reasonable. I told you. This isn't about sides."

Her smile was tight, her eyes hard. "I'm not stupid, Bryce. I wasn't born yesterday. I know exactly what this is about. You've got a hard-on for that little bitch, don't you? Well, you're *welcome* to her! Now get out. Get out and don't come back!"

"Amy, why don't you and Calista come and have lunch with me today?"

Sometimes Amy thought Lorna must be a mind reader. She always seemed to know when Amy was at loose ends. Sundays were especially hard because Amy had the day off, yet she was reluctant to go anywhere. She knew it was paranoia, but she couldn't shake the feeling that no matter how far away she was in miles, Cole's arms and influence might still reach her. "We'd love to."

An hour later, with Calista settled happily playing with Bear and Buttercup on the kitchen floor, Lorna motioned for Amy to follow her into the living room. "She'll be okay," she said when Amy seemed reluctant. "I just need to tell you something, and little pitchers have big ears."

Once they were out of Calista's earshot, Lorna said, "You're never going to believe this."

"What?"

"Tara threw Bryce out of her house and told him to never come back!"

Amy's mouth dropped open. "Why?" she whispered, although she knew Calista couldn't hear them.

"Apparently you're the cause," Lorna said with a grin.

"Me!"

"Yes, you." Lorna went on to relate what had happened between Bryce and Tara. "Now, mind you," she said when she'd finished, "this is what he told me. There could be more that he didn't say."

"When did this happen?"

"Last night."

"How'd you know about it so soon?"

"He drove by here on his way home, saw my lights were still on and stopped to talk to me about it."

"Is he upset?"

"Well, he hates to have any bad feelings between them, because it's bound to affect the rest of the family. Other than that, I'm not sure he cares that much.''

"I knew she was trying to discredit me," Amy said. Part of her felt sorry for Tara, who must have felt desperate to resort to doing what she had and who now was probably humiliated and hurt by the consequences. But the other part of Amy—the secret, not-so-nice part of her— wanted to shoot her fist into the air in triumph and yell, "Take *that,* Tara."

"I think my brother likes you," Lorna said.

"Well, I should hope so. I'd hate to think he disliked me."

"I don't mean in that way, you dunce. I mean *likes* you, as in covets your bod."

"Lorna!" Amy knew she was blushing and could have kicked herself. "What a thing to say."

"Why?" said Lorna innocently. "It's the truth. And I think it's *great!* It's about time he started feeling normal urges again."

Oh, Lord, Amy thought. *How am I ever going to look Bryce in the eye again?*

"Now tell me the truth," Lorna said. The sly grin was back. "You feel the same way about *him,* don't you?"

"Lorna!" Amy exclaimed again. "What's gotten *into* you?"

"Hey, I've got eyes in my head. I see the way he looks at you. And I see the way you avoid looking at him. I just put one and one together."

Amy couldn't think what to say. It was true that she was strongly attracted to Bryce. And yes, if she were being completely honest with herself, she would admit that the thought of sharing a bed with Bryce had crossed her mind—more than once—but she'd ruthlessly pushed it out. But there was no way, no way at all, that she would admit this to anyone. Not even Lorna. Because the bottom line was, it was never going to happen. Bryce might not be in love with Tara, but when he married again, it would be to someone like Tara. Someone of his own class and background. Someone who wasn't lying to him about her past.

If the opportunity for sex with Bryce ever presented itself, and Amy succumbed to desire, she would be committing a huge mistake. A mistake that could only lead to heartache and the loss of her job and her and Calista's safe haven.

"Your brother is very attractive," she said now, finally composed enough to give the only answer she could give, "and any woman would be flattered to have him notice her, but I am his employee. I know this, and he knows this. That's the extent of our relationship."

"Jeez, Amy, you sound like something out of Jane Austen. This is the twenty-first century. Haven't you ever watched *Sex and the City* or *Friends?* Those old-fashioned ideas of yours went out with high-buttoned shoes. If they ever existed,'' Lorna added dryly.

"Proper behavior never goes out of style.'' Even as Amy said it, she realized how prissy she sounded. If only she could tell Lorna the truth about herself.

"Bullhonky to *proper* behavior, as you put it. Bryce is a virile and red-blooded man, and I *think* you're a red-blooded woman.''

"But, Lorna, can't you see that a personal relationship between Bryce and me would be totally wrong.''

"Why? You're two consenting adults.''

"Yes, but Bryce is my employer. What would happen once the, um, affair was over? I'd have to leave. And I don't want to leave.''

"Mommee! Where are you?''

"I'm right here, sweetheart.''

Lorna had no choice but to drop the subject, and Amy was glad. But later, after Amy and Calista left for home, she thought about the things Lorna had said. *Was* Bryce attracted to her? Even the thought caused her heart to beat faster.

That night she had an erotic dream, one in which she and Bryce were entwined in his bed and he was making slow, passionate love to her.

She woke up just as the pink light of dawn crept into the eastern sky. Lying there, still shaken by her dream, she knew that unless she did something about it, she was heading for disaster, because if Bryce made any move toward her, any move at all, she doubted she would have the strength to resist.

Why did he have to be such a great guy?

It would be so easy to fall in love with him.

It would be so easy to get her heart broken.

Oh, Amy, Amy, she lectured herself. *Don't dare go down this path. Don't even think about going down this path. Don't delude yourself that it could possibly end any way but badly. You know there's no chance you could ever have any kind of future with Bryce Hathaway. He might not be in love with Tara, but if and when he marries again, it will be to someone like Tara, and you know it.*

Maybe Amy should just call it quits right now. Make up some excuse, give Bryce her notice, then head for points west the way she'd initially planned.

But even the thought of doing so filled her with despair, not just for her own sake, but also for Calista's. If Amy pulled up stakes and left Texas, Calista would be heartbroken. She loved living in Morgan Creek. In just a few short weeks she had become very close to Bryce's daughters.

Hadn't Calista suffered enough trauma with first the divorce, then the abrupt flight from Mobile? Did Amy have the right to inflict any more pain and suffering on her child?

No, she didn't.

She needed to tough it out. She was a mature adult, capable of exercising restraint and willpower. Just because she was attracted to Bryce didn't mean she ever had to acknowledge it to him or act upon that attraction.

She had a choice.

She just had to make sure she made the right one.

Bryce decided not to wait to talk to Susan. On Tuesday he called Lorna and asked her if she'd invite Stella to do something with her that evening so he could take Susan out to dinner. "I'm going to talk to her about what Tara told her. See if I can't reassure her about things."

"And what if she won't talk to you?"

"I'll cross that bridge when I come to it."

"She might not, Bryce. She's only seven."

"I know, but I have to try."

"Okay. I'll call and talk to Stella."

"What I thought I'd do is tell the girls I want us to occasionally have time alone together, just two of us, and that tonight will be Susan's turn and next week will be Stella's."

Next Bryce called Amy to let her know she'd only have herself and Calista to feed that evening.

Susan was delighted to be singled out. Bryce hoped Stella wasn't hurt not to be first, especially as Susan couldn't keep from bragging.

"I don't care," he heard Stella say. "Aunt Lorna said *we're* going to do something special tonight."

He couldn't help but smile. Maybe Stella was growing out from under Susan's influence.

He made arrangements to drop Stella at Lorna's on their way. She bounced out of the car happily and waved goodbye from Lorna's front porch. "Okay, toots," he said to Susan as he backed out of Lorna's driveway. "Where do you want to go?"

"Yolanda's," she said without hesitation.

Both he and his girls were hooked on Mexican food. "That's where I wanted to go, too."

He was glad to see the restaurant was only about half-full, so it wouldn't be too noisy nor would the owners be anxious to move people in and out quickly.

Once they'd placed their orders and had their drinks and a basket of warm chips and a bowl of salsa to enjoy, Bryce casually said, "How are you and Miss Hudson getting along?" Miss Hudson was Susan's second-grade teacher.

"Good."

"Just good?"

"Uh-huh." Susan was mumbling around a mouthful of chips.

"So you like her?"

"Uh-huh." Susan reached for several more chips.

Bryce could see this wasn't going to be easy. Susan, who was normally a chatterbox, had suddenly become subdued.

"What about Miss Amy? Do you like her?"

Susan looked at him.

He looked back. Maybe if he didn't elaborate, she would open up. A long twenty seconds passed. When Bryce was just about to give up and prod her with another question, she said, "She's okay."

"I think she's more than okay, Susan. I like her."

Susan shrugged and reached for more chips.

"Honey, I know you like Miss Amy, too."

Susan took a long drink of her soda and eyed him over the rim of the plastic glass.

"And you like Calista," he continued doggedly.

For the first time since Bryce had initiated the discussion, Susan perked up. "She's funny."

Bryce smiled. This was better. "She's a nice little girl, and I know she really likes you and Stella. Miss Amy told me that Calista is very happy here with us."

"She likes to play with me and Stella."

Bryce ate a couple of chips. He kept his tone offhand. "Do you like having Miss Amy as your nanny?"

Another shrug.

Bryce felt as if he were pulling teeth. "I think she's really nice."

Silence.

"Susan, Tara told me something the other day."

Susan's eyes met his.

"She said you two were talking and you were afraid Miss Amy was going to leave. Is that true?"

Susan looked away.

"Susan?"

She didn't answer for a long moment. When her gaze met his again, it contained something that made him want to reach out and hold her close. "She *is* going to leave."

"Why do you say that, honey?"

"'Cause she is."

"There must be a reason you think so. Did Miss Amy tell you she was leaving?"

She shook her head.

"Did Calista say something?" he pressed.

Another head shake.

Bryce decided silence might be best at this point.

Finally Susan said, "Tara said Miss Amy was going to leave."

"Well, honey, Tara was wrong. Neither Miss Amy nor Calista is going to leave."

"I don't like having a nanny."

Although what Susan had said might seem like a non sequitur, Bryce knew it wasn't, and he was glad they finally seemed to be getting down to some honest feelings. Unfortunately, the words were barely out of Susan's mouth when their waiter appeared with their food, so Bryce couldn't immediately respond. But once their plates were set before them and their waiter had refilled their glasses and finally gone away again, Bryce said, "Why did you say you don't like having a nanny?"

"I'm not a baby!"

"I know you're not, but you and Stella aren't old enough to be on your own when I'm not there."

"Why can't you just get a baby-sitter, then? Why do we have to have a *nanny* living with us?" She said *nanny* as if it were a nasty word.

"Because I don't always know when I'm going to be gone. I can't do everything myself, honey. You know that. I need to know that someone trustworthy is there to look after you and your sister when I can't be."

"Nannies are for babies." So saying, she attacked her enchilada, venting her frustration the only way she could.

"So you want Miss Amy to leave, is that it?"

Susan kept eating and didn't answer.

"Susan, you do realize that if Miss Amy leaves Calista will be leaving, too?"

That got her attention. She stared at him.

"I don't think you want that, do you?"

She shook her head. She looked miserable. Maybe he should just make an appointment with her doctor and see about getting them some family counseling. It was obvious Susan had some contradictory feelings regarding Amy.

Sounds familiar, Bryce thought wryly. After all, he, too, had contradictory feelings toward Amy, and he didn't have the excuse of youth to justify his own inability to resolve them.

For a while after that they ate in silence.

"Susan," Bryce finally said, "honey, I want you and your sister to be happy. And I think you *are* happier now. I think you like Miss Amy and Calista living with us." Bryce hoped he wasn't just wishing aloud.

Susan's eyes, so like Michelle's in their avid curiosity about the world around them, met his steadily.

"But I also think maybe there are things that bother you," he continued gently, "and that we should talk about them. I know there are things that bother me, and I'll bet Stella has things that bother her. So maybe you and I and Stella need to start talking about our feelings."

"You mean like have a meeting? Jessica's family has a family meeting every Sunday night." Jessica Dalzell was Susan's best friend at school.

"They do, huh?"

She nodded. "They sit around the kitchen table and they vote on stuff."

"Like a family council." That was an interesting idea.

"Jessica said they all get to say what they think."

"Would you like to do something like that?"

"Uh-huh. It'd be cool."

"What about if we did that with someone else?"

She frowned. "Who?"

"A counselor. Somebody who knows a lot about families and would help us work out our problems."

"Not Miss Amy."

"No, not Miss Amy. A doctor."

Susan thought about that for a while. Then she grinned. "A shrink."

Bryce laughed. "Where'd you learn about shrinks?"

"Bobby Landis goes to a shrink. He said it's cool."

"So you like the idea?"

"Uh-huh."

"Think Stella will?"

Susan gave him a look as if to say, *If I like it, she will.*

All in all, Bryce thought as they drove home, he was pretty happy with the way their talk had gone. Maybe they hadn't dug into Susan's feelings about losing Michelle, but that would come later under the guidance of someone much more qualified to deal with any resultant revelations than Bryce.

He decided he would call the girls' pediatrician tomorrow. He should have taken this action a long time ago. Why hadn't he? Why had he listened to his mother when he'd known he and the children were in trouble?

It had taken a stranger to show him what needed doing. Amazing how many ways Amy's entrance into their lives had changed them. He felt he was finally leaving the dark days behind, and he was confident his girls would, too.

Chapter Nine

About an hour after Bryce and the girls left the house, a call came for him.

"I'm sorry," Amy told the woman caller, "but Mr. Hathaway isn't home this evening. Would you like to leave a message for him?"

"What about Stella and Susan?" the woman asked. "This is Pauline Stockbridge, the girls' grandmother. And I'm guessing you're the new nanny."

"Yes, I'm Amy. Amy Gordon."

"Well, it's nice to meet you, Amy, even if it's only on the telephone."

"Thank you. You, too. And in answer to your question, no the girls aren't here, either. Bryce...um,

Mr. Hathaway...took Susan out to dinner, and Stella is spending the evening with her aunt Lorna.''

''Oh?''

Amy could tell just by Michelle's mother's tone of voice that she found this to be a curious arrangement, but Amy didn't feel it was her place to explain.

''In that case, would you please tell Bryce I called and ask him to call me?''

''I'll be happy to.''

''Thank you, Amy. I trust we'll meet in person one of these days.''

''I'm looking forward to it.''

Amy hung up thoughtfully. She wondered what Mrs. Stockbridge was like. She'd sounded nice, if a bit formal. Amy didn't know a lot about Michelle's parents—only what Lorna had told her and a couple of things the girls had mentioned. She knew they lived in Georgetown, which was about half an hour's drive north of Austin and that they spent a good part of each summer in England where Mr. Stockbridge had inherited a family estate.

They were back home now, obviously, and Amy assumed they probably wanted to come down to see the girls. Lorna had told her they were crazy about both of them. That Michelle had been their only child and so Susan and Stella were their only grandchildren.

The thought of having Michelle's parents there made Amy nervous. What if they didn't like her?

What if they told Bryce she wasn't suitable? What if they encouraged him to get rid of her?

Oh, for heaven's sake. She was being ridiculous. What was her problem? Why did she always think of the worst thing that could happen instead of focusing on positive things?

She was still wrestling with her fears when the doorbell rang. Amy looked at her watch. It was after eight. Who could that be? No one had rung to say a visitor was on the way, so it must be someone from the main house. Amy grimaced. She hoped it wasn't Bryce's mother. Amy hadn't spent much time around Kathleen, but the time she had spent with her hadn't been comfortable. Amy wasn't sure why. Bryce's mother was perfectly polite, but Amy knew the older woman wasn't entirely sold on her. It was as if Kathleen Hathaway sensed that Amy wasn't all she seemed to be.

"Mommy, somebody's here," Calista said, looking up from her coloring book.

"I know, sweetie. You sit here while I go see who it is, okay?"

"'Kay."

When Amy reached the front door, she was relieved to discover Bryce's youngest sister on the doorstep. "Hi, Claudia. Come on in."

"Hi, Amy. Is Bryce around?"

Amy explained where he'd gone and why. "They

should be home soon, I would think. They left about six-thirty.''

"Do you mind if I wait for him?"

"Of course not." Amy had been about to take Calista upstairs and start her bath, but it didn't matter if they waited. "Calista's out in the kitchen. Want to come out and have something to drink?"

"Sure."

As Amy poured iced tea for them both, she covertly studied Claudia. Tonight the younger woman wore low-riding cargo pants with a couple of layered tank tops, the outer one black, the inner one pink. Black clogs, an armful of chunky black and silver bracelets, and two black barrettes haphazardly holding back her spiky hair completed her costume. On her the outfit looked great. Trendy and young and casually chic. If Amy had worn something similar, she'd have looked ludicrous. Oh, well, she thought. Better not to try to be something she wasn't. The irony of that thought wasn't lost on her.

"So how're things working out for you?" Claudia asked.

"Mommy, I want something to drink!"

"Calista, it's not polite to interrupt."

Calista frowned, and Amy was afraid she was going to have one of her little temper tantrums again, but all she did was sigh heavily, the way she'd seen Amy sigh when she was exasperated. "But I'm thirsty, too."

Amy glanced at Claudia, and she could see Claudia was trying not to laugh. "All right. I'll pour you some milk."

"I want Dr. Pepper."

"Sorry. No Dr. Pepper tonight."

Thankfully, Calista didn't argue. Amy poured her milk, then invited Claudia to sit down. "You asked how things were going. They're going well, I think. Calista and I really like it here, and I think the girls like us, too."

"I'm so glad. It's been tough for Bryce and the girls the past few years."

"Yes, I know."

Claudia drank some of her tea. She smiled at Amy. "We all think the world of Bryce."

"He's a good guy."

"The best." Claudia fiddled with her napkin. "I used to think it was normal for brothers to be like Bryce, but in college I discovered how lucky we really are, because I got to know girls whose brothers weren't supportive or understanding or generous or any of the things Bryce is."

"You *are* lucky."

"We all come running to him when things go wrong."

"He's easy to talk to."

"That's because he actually *listens*. Do you know how few men actually listen?"

"Oh, yes." Cole had never heard a thing Amy said.

"So here I am," Claudia said dryly. "Ready to cry on his shoulder once again."

"Did something happen?"

"It's what *didn't* happen that's got me down." She made a face. "I didn't get the job I wanted."

"Oh, I'm sorry."

"Yeah, me, too." Morosely, Claudia drew circles in the condensation on her glass.

"There'll be other jobs," Amy said kindly.

"Yeah, I know. That's what Bryce will say, too. But I really, really wanted this one."

"Is that the one with the college in Houston?"

Claudia looked up in surprise. "Bryce told you about that?"

"Actually, I think Lorna told me."

"Oh, of course. I keep forgetting you and Lorna are good friends."

Just then Amy heard the garage door opening. "Bryce is home." She finished her tea and stood. "Calista, honey, it's time to go and have your bath." She smiled at Claudia. "I've really enjoyed talking to you."

"Me, too. Say, maybe you and I and Lorna can catch a movie together sometime. My brother lets you out occasionally, doesn't he?"

"Yes, but there's Calista…"

"Oh, I'm so stupid. Of course. You'd need a baby-sitter. We'll figure it out."

Just then the back door opened and Bryce and Susan walked in. "Hey, Claudia."

"Hey, bro." Claudia bent down and gave Susan a hug. "Hey, Suze."

"Hi, Aunt Claudia."

"Bryce, I was just telling Amy here that I was sure you wouldn't mind baby-sitting Calista some night so she could go to the movies with me and Lorna."

Amy was dumbfounded. Her gaze flew to Bryce's. "Oh, I couldn't possibly—"

"Sure, no problem," Bryce said.

When he smiled at her like that, Amy's knees felt weak.

Claudia smiled triumphantly. "See? I told you we'd figure it out."

"Um, Bryce, while you were gone, Mrs. Stockbridge called. She wants you to call her."

"Okay. Thanks."

Later, after Amy had taken Calista upstairs and given her her bath and was tucking her into bed, she thought about how happy they both were and how safe they felt now.

Please God, she prayed, *please help me stay strong and not do anything to jeopardize my job. Please keep us safe from harm and out of Cole's reach.*

Bending down, she smoothed Calista's hair back from her forehead and kissed her. "Love you, sweetie."

"Love you, too." Calista frowned. "Mommy?"

"Yes, sweetheart?"

"Mommy, are we going home?"

Amy's heart knocked against her chest. For a moment she was at a loss. Since Calista hadn't mentioned going home before, Amy had almost begun to think the child had forgotten all about home and her father. "Do...do you want to go home, honey?"

Calista stared up at Amy. "No," she said in a small voice.

Amy wished it wasn't necessary to continue questioning Calista, yet she knew she must. Her child was confused and probably frightened by things she didn't understand. It was Amy's responsibility to try to reassure her and put her fears at rest. "Would you be sad if we never went home?"

"I don't know."

Okay, Amy, this is going to be the hard part. Taking a deep breath, she said gently, "Do you miss your daddy, Calista?"

At first Calista didn't answer. Then, almost defiantly, she said, "No! Daddy doesn't like me."

Part of Amy was relieved. The other part was sad. No part of her was surprised. The fact that Calista hadn't talked about Cole once had only reinforced what Amy knew in her heart.

Cole didn't care about Calista. Never had.

Amy could only imagine how many nights and weekends Calista had spent in Mrs. Witherspoon's care, totally ignored by her father. No wonder Calista felt as she did. But how terrible that any child had been made to feel this way. "Of course he likes you, sweetheart."

"No, he doesn't!" Calista's eyes welled with tears. "He *hates* me."

"No, Calista, he doesn't hate you."

"He does! He does!"

"Okay, okay. Calm down. Listen to me, honey." Amy gathered Calista in her arms and held her close. She kissed the top of her head. "There's nothing to worry about. Mommy's here, and you're here, and we're going to stay here for a long time. Okay?"

"P-p-promise?"

"I promise."

Calista sniffed. "I don't wanna go home."

"We won't. I promise. Now go to sleep, precious." Amy gently laid Calista back on her pillow and kissed her again.

"'Kay."

Amy forced herself to smile reassuringly and lighten her voice. "Sleep tight..."

Tears dry now, Calista giggled. "An' don't let the bedbugs bite."

Looking down at her troubled and trusting daughter, Amy wondered how she could have even considered doing anything that might jeopardize her position here.

And yet, as she softly closed the door behind her and headed for her own bedroom, she couldn't help remembering the way Bryce had smiled at her when he'd come in tonight.

Why couldn't I have met him before I met Cole?

Of course, she thought dryly, Bryce wouldn't have looked twice at her before. It was only because he needed her that she was here at all.

This story isn't going to have a fairy-tale ending. You are not Cinderella and he is not Prince Charming. He is your employer—a rich, eligible man who is so far removed from the likes of you that you might as well be from different planets.

And don't you forget it.

"Mr. Hathaway?"

Bryce looked up from the notes he'd made in preparation for the meeting with his brother-in-law about the new Hathaway ad campaign. "Yes, Lisa?"

"Your mother's here to see you."

"Here?" Bryce couldn't remember the last time his mother had visited the plant.

Lisa, Bryce's longtime secretary, nodded.

From her expression, Bryce knew she was just as surprised as he was. "Give me a second, then send her in." Bryce hoped whatever his mother wanted wouldn't take too long. It was already ten-thirty and his brother-in-law Greg, along with the art director from his agency, were due to arrive at eleven.

A minute later, Bryce's mother walked briskly into his office. As always, Kathleen Bryce Hathaway looked impeccable. Today she wore a dark-rose suit paired with a pale-pink blouse. A diamond *H* pin adorned her lapel. Bryce stood and kissed her cheek. "Good morning. You look lovely today."

"Thank you, dear."

She smiled, but the smile seemed strained to Bryce.

"To what do I owe the honor of this visit?"

She walked over to the grouping of chairs around a low coffee table in the sunny southeast corner of Bryce's office and sat. Bryce followed her, taking the chair opposite her.

"I was going to call you," she began. "Then I decided this was too important to discuss on the phone. And I certainly didn't want to discuss it at your house."

"Oh?"

"I am terribly upset, Bryce. Terribly."

"I'm sorry to hear that, Mother. What happened?"

"You know very well what happened."

Tara, Bryce thought in belated awareness.

"I spoke with Tara last night."

Bryce stifled a sigh. He did not want to discuss this subject. He especially did not want to discuss it here or now.

"I just cannot believe what you did."

"Mother…"

"You know, Bryce, I thought you had some sense. But lately I've begun to wonder."

Bryce gritted his teeth. He told himself not to answer, because if he did, he'd probably say something he'd be sorry for later.

"First you hire a woman of whom we know nothing. Then you insult the daughter of your father's and my dearest friend—a woman you grew up with, a woman who only has your best interest at heart, a woman who we all believed you'd mar—"

"That's enough," Bryce said. "I don't need you to tell me who Tara is. I know very well who she is. Now look, Mother, I love you, but there are some lines even you can't cross. And this is one of them." He stood. "I'm sorry, but I have a meeting with Greg and his art director in fifteen minutes. I don't have time to talk anymore."

"If you think I'm leaving before we get this settled, you're quite wrong."

"There is no *we*. What happened between me and Tara is our business, not yours." Bryce walked back to his desk and started reorganizing his notes for the upcoming meeting.

After a moment of silence, she said, "Tara was right. This is all that nanny's doing."

Bryce didn't look up. "Goodbye, Mother." He was determined to stay calm.

"Fine," she said, finally getting up. "I'll leave. But you haven't heard the last of this. I fully intend to talk to your father about your behavior."

Bryce couldn't help it. He started to laugh. "And then what? Is he going to spank me?"

"This isn't funny."

Bryce met her gaze levelly. "No, Mother, it isn't. But what you just said is ludicrous. First of all, I'm a grown man and how I live is my business. Secondly, Dad hasn't taken charge of anything in any of our lives for years. What makes you think he'd care enough to start now?" Bryce threw down the sheaf of papers in his hands. "You know what? I hope Dad *does* show some interest. Maybe then I can get out from under this job, quit shouldering the responsibility for the whole damn family and have a life of my own for a change!"

Every day Amy eagerly looked forward to the mail delivery. Finally, two weeks after sending off the birthday package to her father, she received one in return. The letter had been repackaged in a plain brown envelope with the post office box of the network as the sender. Amy eagerly tore it open and read:

Dearest Amy,
I was so glad to hear from you. I knew you'd taken Calista and fled Mobile, because Cole

paid me a visit a week before your letter and birthday present arrived. More about that later. He was under the mistaken impression I knew where you were, but I very happily disabused him of that notion. I did want to warn you, though. Although he has no idea where you are, he knows you had help getting away because he traced the phone numbers on your phone bill and found out about the underground network. I imagine they're used to dealing with people like him, but I worry about you. I hope you can stay hidden from him because he's furious. He told me to tell you he'll find you eventually and when he does he'll see you in jail and make sure you never see Calista again.

How is my little sweetheart doing? Send me some pictures of her, will you, honey?

Thank you for the robe and slippers. They'll come in handy this winter. My almanac is predicting a colder than normal one.

Amy, my dear, I know you don't like talking about my death, but I'm eighty years old now, and if I've learned anything in all that time, I've learned that death respects no one. I could die tomorrow, and if I do, I want to be sure you're taken care of. I don't have a lot of money, but when the house is sold, there will be a nice little sum for you and Calista.

Anyway, I called that woman, Regina, at the

network, and talked to her about it. She told me
to get all my papers in order, and she'll forward
them on to you. I'm going to tell my lawyer to
call her if something happens to me, and she'll
get in touch with you.

Please don't be sad, Amy. We'll see each
other again, if not here on earth, then in Heaven
someday. I just want you to be safe. You and
Calista. So you stay wherever you are, and don't
worry about me. You'll always be in my
thoughts and prayers.

Amy was crying so hard she could hardly read the
rest of the letter where he'd said they'd write often
and one of these days, when he was sure Cole's
flunky had stopped following him, he'd even call her
if she'd give him the number, and he promised he'd
commit it to memory and never write it down.

At that exact moment, with tears running down her
face and the letter in her hand, Bryce walked in the
back door. He stopped dead when he saw her.

"Amy! What's wrong?" Immediately he was at
her side.

Amy fought to get her emotions under control.
"I...I'm, nothing's wrong. I was just reading a letter
from my f-father and...I'm sorry. I just...I miss
him." She reached for a tissue in the box on the
counter, but found it empty.

"Here," Bryce said, pulling a handkerchief out of his pocket. "It's clean."

"Thanks." Amy blew her nose. Taking a deep breath, she tried to make her voice light. "I'm okay now. I'm sorry I alarmed you."

"Are you sure?" Bryce was standing so close, if Amy leaned forward at all, they would be touching.

"Y-yes." But her voice wobbled, and when her eyes met Bryce's, all she wanted was to throw herself into his arms and have him tell her everything would be okay.

A long moment passed, and then, as if in slow motion, he gathered her into his arms. "Amy," he said, stroking her hair. "I wish—"

Later, Amy wondered what would have happened between them if the phone hadn't rung just then. It only rang once, then stopped—probably a wrong number—but it was enough to make them jump apart.

"I'm sorry, I—" Bryce began.

"No, it's okay." Amy couldn't look at him. Her face felt hot, and her heart was beating too fast.

After a moment Bryce said, "Where does your father live?" Once more he was the solicitous employer, nothing more.

"In Florida." Amy wished she'd had the presence of mind not to read her letter downstairs. To save it until tonight where she would have been in the privacy of her room. But it was too late. She'd read the letter downstairs and been caught crying. And now there would be the inevitable questions, and she'd have to tell more lies.

"How old is he?"

"He just had his eightieth birthday a couple of weeks ago."

"It's hard to be this far from him."

"Yes." She wondered if he was thinking about how she'd originally planned to go to California, where she would have been even farther.

"When's the last time you saw him?"

"I went down there the first week of June."

"You and Calista?"

"Y-yes." Her heart leaped. Oh, God. That old adage about the tangled web we weave when we start telling lies was so true. She'd almost made a costly mistake, forgetting that Bryce would naturally expect her to take Calista to Florida with her.

"You know, Amy, if you want time off to go and visit your father, all you have to do is ask."

Guilt surged through Amy. Bryce was so kind. Such a good man. He didn't deserve to be lied to. "Thank you. I appreciate that." *Even though I'll never be able to take you up on the offer.*

"Is your father in good health?"

"Sometimes his knees give him trouble. He's got a touch of arthritis. But considering his age, he's doing really well."

''If he can travel, you've always got the option of inviting him to come here for a long visit, too.''

With each additional kind and generous offer, he was making her feel worse. Oh, wouldn't it be wonderful if she *could* ask her father to come here? It would be so good for Calista to really get to know her grandfather. Especially as she had no male influence in her life.

And yet Amy knew this was a pipe dream. She could never ask her father to come here. She didn't dare take that chance. Who knew how long Cole would watch her father's movements? Knowing Cole and how single-minded he could be when he wanted something, it might be years before he gave up. Maybe he'd *never* give up.

Suddenly despair filled Amy. Had she been crazy to think she'd ever have a normal life again? It was with a heavy heart that she said good-night to Bryce and went upstairs to collect Calista and get her ready for bed.

Bryce wasn't sure what woke him up at two in the morning, whether it was a noise or whether he'd been dreaming. Whatever the reason, he couldn't seem to get back to sleep. He kept thinking about the visit from his mother and how frustrating she was. Maybe he should have explained to her that Amy wasn't the reason he and Tara had had words. Tara herself was the reason. She was the one who had caused the problem, not Amy.

Amy. He thought about how sad she'd been earlier. He hated seeing her so unhappy and wished he'd been able to think of the right thing to say that might have helped, but nothing he'd offered had seemed to make a difference. For some reason she hadn't leaped at either suggestion. He wondered why, if she missed her father so much, she hadn't just moved to Florida to be close to him. Why head for California?

Of course, he was glad she hadn't. In just a few short weeks she'd become so much a part of his household and his life, he couldn't imagine not having her there.

This thought automatically led to the ugly remark Tara had flung at him Saturday night, that he had a hard-on for Amy. At the time he'd denied it vehemently to himself. But tonight, alone and lonely in his big bed, Bryce finally admitted there was some truth to Tara's accusation. Lately he'd found himself thinking about Amy in ways that had nothing to do with the girls.

Two days earlier, after dinner, when she'd reached up into one of the cabinets, her T-shirt rode up, exposing the flesh above the waistband of her shorts, and Bryce had been shaken by the surge of pure lust he'd felt. And tonight, seeing her in tears, he hadn't been able to stop himself from putting his arms around her.

If the phone hadn't rung, God knows what might have happened, because if he was honest with himself, he'd admit that he hadn't just wanted to comfort her. He'd wanted to kiss her. He'd wanted to kiss her again and again and then bring her back here to his bed and make love to her.

Damn. He'd better be careful. Even if Amy hadn't been an employee—thereby making her off-limits— he knew she wasn't the kind of woman who would take part in a casual affair. So he'd better be sure he was ready for a serious relationship before he made any move in her direction that was anything other than friendship or business.

At three o'clock, still thinking about Amy, Bryce knew he probably wasn't going to fall back to sleep, so he decided to go downstairs, get himself some milk and a few of those chocolate chip cookies Amy had baked the day before, and go into his office and work on the computer for a while.

Even though he knew everyone else was sound asleep and wasn't likely to see him, he put on a robe before going out to the kitchen. He flipped on the overhead light, then opened the refrigerator. There were two containers of milk inside, one full and one with a small amount remaining. He poured the remainder from the older gallon into a glass, decided that was enough for him, then carried the empty plastic container to the waste can. As he was stuffing the container into the trash, he noticed a manila envelope that had been discarded earlier. The return address caught his eye. A post office box number in Mobile, Alabama.

Mobile?

Who had sent something from Mobile?

Curious now, he took the envelope out so he could see the rest of it and saw it was addressed to Amy.

He frowned. Thought back to when he'd come home today and found Amy crying. Had the letter she'd been holding been in an envelope? No. She'd been reading it. He could clearly see the pages loose in her hand. Had she had an envelope, too? He didn't think so. He'd only seen the letter. This envelope must be the one the letter had come in. But if that were so, why was the return address in Mobile if her father lived in Florida?

She's not what she seems to be.

Tara's words. At the time, he'd dismissed them as ridiculous. Prompted by jealousy.

Other things Tara had said came back to him now. *There's something strange about her...something not quite right...what reason could she have for using a pay phone when there's a perfectly good phone at your house?*

No, he thought. What was wrong with him? Why was he suddenly doubting Amy?

There had to be a perfectly reasonable explanation for both the envelope and the phone call. Amy had probably gotten more than one piece of mail today.

The envelope that had contained the letter from her father had probably been in her hand all the time, most likely hidden by the letter itself.

Just because Bryce hadn't seen it didn't mean it wasn't there. And the phone call…that was just what he'd explained to Tara. Amy had been out shopping or running errands, remembered a phone call she needed to make, and stopped at the first place she saw.

Bryce made himself a mental note to get her a cell phone. He'd pay for it. He wanted to be sure that if she had any kind of emergency and wasn't near a phone, she could call him or anyone else she needed to call. He should have thought of doing so long before this.

Relieved that his suspicions had turned out to have no validity, he grabbed a handful of cookies out of the cookie jar, and with his milk and cookies in hand, headed for his office.

Chapter Ten

"I hear you're in trouble with Mom."

"You have my office bugged or something?"

Lorna perched on the edge of Bryce's desk and picked up a paper clip that was lying there. "She called me last night. Gave me an earful." Lorna grimaced. "Now I gather it's all *my* fault."

"Why? Because Amy's *your* friend?"

Lorna unbent the paper clip until it was one long wire. "You got it."

Bryce rolled his eyes. "Hell, it's no damn wonder Claudia wants to leave. There's no privacy around here at all."

Lorna dropped the ruined clip in the wastebasket.

She gave him a thoughtful look. "You scared Mom, you know."

"Really?" Not much scared Kathleen Hathaway.

"Uh-huh. She's afraid you might leave the company. I didn't tell her your threat was empty."

Bryce smiled wryly. "Maybe it wasn't."

"Oh, c'mon, Bryce. We both know you'll never leave. This company is part of you."

"Sometimes I'm tempted."

"I know. That's normal, though. Everyone gets frustrated now and then."

Bryce leaned back in his chair and studied her. "Do you?"

"Of course."

Just then Bryce's phone buzzed. Motioning for Lorna to stay put, Bryce hit the intercom button. "Yes, Lisa?"

"Mr. Hathaway, it's Jack Feegan on line one." Jack Feegan was the plant manager of the El Paso plant.

"Thanks." Bryce pressed the speaker button so that Lorna could hear the conversation. "Jack. Hello."

"Hello, Bryce. I've got bad news."

Bryce sat up straighter.

"The crew went on strike this morning."

Lorna's eyes widened.

"How many are involved?" Bryce asked.

"Everyone in the plant except the managers and Annie." Annie was Jack Feegan's secretary.

Bryce couldn't remember the last time Hathaway Baking Company had had a strike. In fact, the company was known for being a good place to work. They had a low turnover rate and few labor problems. "What the hell happened?"

"They're upset because their health insurance costs went up so much the first of August and because their raises weren't what they expected. They sent a team to see me on Monday. I tried to explain about our costs going up even faster and how we're gettin' hit even worse than they are, but they wouldn't listen. They said they'd voted and if we couldn't do any better than this they were goin' on strike until we could."

"Jesus, Jack, why didn't you call me on Monday?" Bryce's eyes met Lorna's and saw she looked just as concerned as he was.

"I thought I could handle it myself."

"How many orders are pending?"

As Jack gave Bryce the figures, Bryce realized there was no way they could fill the pending orders unless the workers went back almost immediately.

"I'm coming out there," Bryce said. "I'll see about getting a flight out this afternoon."

"Want me to go with you?" Lorna asked when Bryce had disconnected the call.

Bryce shook his head. "You'd better stay here. I'll

take Midge.'' Midge Allen was their human resources manager.

Lorna nodded. ''She'll be more valuable to you,
anyway. Jeez, Bryce, this is bad.''

''You're telling me.''

As soon as Lorna left his office, Bryce had Lisa
check into flights for him, then he called Amy.

''I wanted to give you a heads-up,'' he said when
she answered. ''I have to leave tonight for El Paso.
The plant workers there have gone on strike.''

''Oh. All right.''

''I'm not sure how long I'll be gone. A day. Two.
Maybe more.''

''What do you need me to do to help?''

Bryce appreciated how calm Amy always was.
Nothing he ever said or did caused her to get flus-
tered. She just dealt with whatever crisis there happened to be. ''You know the girls are going to their
Stockbridge grandparents' home for the long weekend.'' Friday was an in-service day for the teachers
at the girls' school, and Mr. and Mrs. Stockbridge
were coming Friday morning to take the girls back
to Georgetown with them.

''Yes, I know.''

''You'll have to get their things packed and have
them ready to go.''

''Of course. I'd planned to do that, anyway.''

He smiled. ''You're a gem, Amy. I don't know
how we managed without you.''

For the next two hours, Bryce was too busy finalizing his plans and clearing some things hanging fire there in Morgan Creek to think about much else, but as he drove home at noon to pack and leave for the airport, he thought again about how lucky he was to have Amy. The previous nannies had all been capable women, and he hadn't worried leaving the girls in their care, but Amy never acted as if he were imposing on her when he needed her to do something outside her normal responsibilities. She just adapted, putting his daughters' needs first without mention of comp time or extra money. He trusted her so completely, it was almost as if she were another member of the family.

When he arrived at the house, Amy and Calista were eating lunch. It gave him a good feeling to see them there in his kitchen. Amy wiped her mouth on her napkin and stood to greet him. She smiled, and he thought how pretty she looked today in her snug-fitting jeans and bright red T-shirt. Her thick hair was tied back with a red ribbon, and if he hadn't known she was in her thirties, he'd have pegged her for no older than twenty-five with her fresh-scrubbed, all-American good looks.

"I just came home to pack," he explained.

"Would you like some lunch before you leave? We're just having tuna sandwiches."

Bryce looked at the clock. "I'm not sure I have time."

"How about if I fix you a sandwich to take along with you?"

"That would be great."

She smiled. "Good. Oh, and after you called, I asked Billy to go to the cleaner's and pick up your dry cleaning."

"You're wonderful, Amy. You know that?"

Her face flushed with pleasure, and Bryce had to fight the sudden urge to lean over and plant a kiss on those soft-looking lips of hers. Even the thought of kissing her sent a stab of longing through him. Unnerved, Bryce mumbled something about how he'd better get started and strode off toward the master bedroom.

"Jeez, Hathaway, get yourself under control," he muttered as he opened his suitcase and started throwing things in. He knew his feelings toward Amy weren't sensible. It was bad news to get involved with an employee. If Amy had been working at the plant, he'd have avoided her like the plague, because Bryce knew better than most how disastrous it could be to get involved with someone who worked for you. It was one thing if the relationship worked out well, but quite another if it didn't. All he had to do was remember what had happened with Scott Jenson and Carey Higgins. Scott had been Bryce's sales manager, and Carey was a young college graduate Scott had hired. The two soon began a torrid affair, but Carey lost interest after a month or two and tried to break it off. Scott didn't take it well. The situation deteriorated to the point where Bryce ended by having to fire both of them.

Learn from that, he told himself.

Yet the image of Amy, so delectable and sexy even as she was wholesome and sweet, wouldn't leave him alone.

Once he'd finished his packing, he carried his suitcase and his laptop out to the kitchen. Amy was wiping Calista's mouth and hands with a washcloth and turned to smile at him. "Your lunch is on the counter," she said.

Bryce's gaze lingered on her as she bent back to her task.

"Can I go play upstairs, Mommy?" Calista asked in her sweet piping voice as Amy finished cleaning her up.

"Sure."

Grinning, Calista ran off. He could hear the pounding of her sneakers as she raced down the hall, then up the stairs.

Bryce reached for the brown bag containing his lunch. Amy's gaze met his. Upstairs, he could hear Calista moving about. In the kitchen the refrigerator hummed, the wall clock ticked. Outside, a blue jay squawked noisily, and somewhere in the distance, a car backfired.

Bryce's heart beat faster as his gaze clung to Amy's. She had the most incredible eyes. A man could fall into those eyes and never want to come out.

I should leave now.

Afterward, he could never think how it happened. All he knew was he fully intended to say goodbye and the next minute he was kissing her. Not a peck, either. A real kiss. One that made his head swim and every hormone in his body leap to attention.

Holy crow! he thought as he raised his head and they stared at each other. *What have I done?*

Then, because he couldn't think what to say, he didn't say anything. He just walked out.

Amy was stunned. She stood in the kitchen just staring at the door after Bryce left.

He'd kissed her!

He'd *kissed* her.

She touched her lips, which still tingled from his. It felt as if her heart was turning summersaults in her chest.

He'd *kissed* her.

What did it mean?

Amy didn't know whether to be thrilled or scared to death. Actually, she was both, she realized. Thrilled *and* scared.

She spent the rest of the day in a daze.

Luckily, Bryce and Midge Allen weren't sitting together—they'd booked their flight at the last minute, necessitating seats apart—so Bryce had plenty of time to think after boarding.

And think he did.

He couldn't figure out what the hell had happened in his kitchen. Either he'd had a temporary blackout during which he'd kissed Amy or he'd lost his mind. But what difference did it make why he'd done it?

The question was, What now?

It wasn't as if he could just go home and pretend that kiss hadn't happened.

You're playing with fire.

By the time his flight landed in El Paso, Bryce had a pounding headache and he was no closer to a solution about where to go from there than he had been when he'd boarded the plane.

But he had to push thoughts of Amy out of his mind when he saw Jack Feegan waiting for him and Midge. They all headed outside where a car and driver waited. As they drove toward the plant, Jack explained what Bryce would find when he got there.

"They're picketing, and Channels 7 and 9—those are the ABC and NBC affiliates—have crews outside."

"Did you talk to them?" Bryce asked.

"Who? The TV people?"

"Yes."

"No. I told them our VP of Operations was coming and you'd talk to them."

"Good." Not that Bryce *wanted* to talk to reporters, but better him than Jack, who wasn't the soul of tact and had a tendency to blurt things out he later regretted.

It was a thirty-minute drive to the plant, and by the time they arrived, Bryce was ready. He still wasn't sure what he could do to placate the employees and get them back to work, but as someone much wiser than he had once said, the buck stopped at his desk.

"Why didn't Daddy wait until we got home?" Susan asked.

Amy answered patiently, even though she'd already answered this question three times already. "Honey, I told you. He couldn't. There was a big problem at one of the plants and he had to fly there this afternoon."

Susan scowled. "He should have waited. Miss Hudson said only our parents can sign our spelling papers."

"I know, but this is a special case. I'll sign your father's name for him and send along a note for your teacher explaining that he's out of town."

Susan stamped her foot. "I don't want *you* to sign my paper!"

Amy counted to ten. For some reason Susan was in a terrible mood this afternoon, and ever since she'd come home from school had been trying to pick a fight with Amy.

"You can sign *my* paper," Stella said.

Amy smiled at the older girl. "Thank you, Stella."

"You're a *suck-up*," Susan said, giving Stella a push that caught her unaware and caused her to lose her balance. She would have fallen if Amy hadn't grabbed for her.

"Susan!" Amy said. "That was uncalled for. Go to your room. You're in time out."

"I don't have to."

Please, God. Don't let me lose my temper. "Yes, you do have to. When your father isn't here, I'm in charge."

"I'm going to call my grandmother," Susan retorted. But she marched out of the kitchen and Amy could hear her stomping up the stairs a few seconds later.

What gets into that kid? Amy wondered. For the past few days, ever since Bryce had taken her out to dinner and talked to her, she'd been sunny and sweet and a model of good behavior. And now this. Was her acting out a reaction to her father's absence? Or was it something else?

"What would you two like to do?" Amy asked brightly.

"Wanna play with Play-Doh?" Stella asked Calista.

"Yeah! Play-Doh!" Calista shouted.

"Okay." With Stella's help, Amy carried the cans of Play-Doh from the pantry and put them on the kitchen table. Soon the two girls were happily mold-ing the colored clay.

"I'm going up to talk to Susan," Amy said to Stella. "I'm counting on you two to play nicely while I'm upstairs."

"Okay, Miss Amy," Stella said. She put her arm around Calista's shoulders. "I'll watch Calista."

"Thank you."

A few moments later Amy tapped lightly upon Su-san's closed bedroom door. She didn't answer. "Su-san?" she called. "May I come in?"

Still no answer.

Amy waited a few seconds, then turned the door-knob. When she entered the bedroom, she found Su-san lying facedown on the bed. Her shoulders were shaking.

Amy's tender heart smote her. "Susan, honey..." Amy sat on the side of the bed and gently rubbed Susan's back. "I'm sorry I had to punish you. Can we talk?"

"I don't want to talk to you."

Amy could barely make out the words, since Su-san didn't raise her head.

Amy waited a couple of seconds. "You know, Su-san, when I came here, I was worried that maybe you and Stella wouldn't like me. And I wanted you to like me. Not just because I wanted this job as your nanny, but because I liked *you*. I thought you espe-cially were such a cool kid. I could see that you were smart and funny and interesting. And I haven't changed my mind about that. So it hurts me that you don't seem to want me to be here.'' She could have added *complicated* and *frustrating* to the adjectives, but those were better left unsaid.

Susan didn't answer for a long moment. Finally she rolled over and sat up. Her blue eyes, the exact color of Bryce's, met Amy's levelly. ''You think I'm *cool?*'' she finally said.

Amy smiled. ''Yes.'' She could see Susan wanted to smile back but was fighting the temptation.

''I want you to be here,'' Susan said after a while.

''Then why do you fight me so much?''

Susan shrugged. ''I don't know.''

Amy wished she could hug the girl—who seemed so desperately to need something she wasn't getting—but she didn't want to push her luck.

And then Susan surprised her. The child leaned forward and put her arms around Amy. With a rush of warmth and love, Amy hugged Susan back.

''I'm sorry I talked back,'' Susan murmured against Amy's chest.

''It's forgotten. Now why don't we go downstairs? Stella and Calista are playing with Play-Doh.''

As they walked down the stairs together, Amy felt that somehow, today, she and Susan had turned a corner. She only hoped that what had happened earlier between her and Bryce wouldn't completely wipe away that gain.

* * *

After Susan and Stella left with their Stockbridge grandparents on Friday morning, Calista cried for more than an hour. Amy was at her wit's end. Even after Calista finally stopped crying, she moped around and whined and didn't want to do anything except cling to Amy.

By five o'clock, Amy was ready to tear her hair out. When Lorna called and asked how things were going, Amy blurted out her frustration. "I don't know what to *do* with her!" she ended, now sounding as whiny as her daughter.

"Why don't I come and get her?" Lorna offered. "I'll take her out for pizza and ice cream, and then she can come and have a sleepover at my house, just like Stella and Susan are having at their grandparents' house. And you can have a whole night to yourself. You can soak in the tub and give yourself a manicure and pedicure and anything else you feel like doing."

"Oh, Lorna!" Amy wanted to say yes, but she felt she should at least offer a token protest. "That's so nice of you, but I couldn't do that to you."

"But I *want* to have her. I adore Calista. You know that. And I never have her to myself. It'll be a treat for me, too."

Amy almost danced when they hung up the phone. And Calista was just as delighted when Amy told her Aunt Lorna was coming to get her. She raced upstairs to get her bag packed, and Amy even allowed her to pick out her own clothes to wear tomorrow. Bear had to go into the backpack, too, and so did two of her dolls. Then Calista, who wouldn't let Amy carry the backpack, lugged it downstairs and sat on the bottom step waiting for Lorna to arrive.

Twenty minutes later she did.

"You're a saint, you know," Amy told Lorna as she handed over her daughter.

"That's me, Saint Lorna," said Lorna, laughing.

Amy kissed Calista goodbye and stood out on the driveway and waved until she couldn't see the car anymore. Then she walked back inside, locked the door, and headed straight for the bar in the living room. After pouring herself a glass of wine, she headed for her bedroom.

Three hours later, with a pleasant buzz from two glasses of wine, and feeling wonderful with her squeaky-clean, fragrant skin and her freshly painted nails and toes, Amy walked slowly down the stairs. She was naked under her loosely belted terry cloth robe and her hair hung in wet ringlets, but it didn't matter. There was no one to see her.

She went into the living room and looked through Bryce's CDs, finally settling on Puccini's *Madame Butterfly,* which had always affected Amy deeply. She turned the sound up high and, humming along, was trying to decide whether she wanted to fix herself something to eat or whether she wanted another glass of wine.

What the heck? she thought. Why not have both?

With a fresh glass in her hand, she padded out to the hall and walked straight into Bryce.

Amy screamed and nearly dropped her wine. As it was, some of it splattered over the edge of the glass and landed on his shirt. "Ohmigod! You scared me!"

"I'm sorry," Bryce said. He put his suitcase and laptop down on the floor. "I tried to call you, but there was no answer."

"I...I was taking a bath. I guess I didn't hear the phone."

Bryce's gaze lowered, and suddenly Amy was aware of just how she looked. Her own gaze dropped, and she belatedly realized how her robe now gaped open, revealing her naked breasts almost to the nipples. When she looked up again, her eyes met his.

"Amy..." His voice sounded raspy, not like his at all.

And then, as her heart pounded like a crazed thing, he took the wineglass from her hands and set it on the table in the foyer. Then he drew her into his arms, lowered his head, and kissed her.

Amy's head spun. The kiss went on and on. Became two kisses. Then three. His tongue delved, tangling with hers, as his hands untied the belt around her waist, then slowly slipped inside to caress her bare skin.

Amy moaned when they found her breasts, the thumbs stroking back and forth across her rigid nipples.

When Bryce, with a moan of his own, scooped her up and into his arms and carried her back into his bedroom, she didn't protest. She couldn't. She wanted him as badly as she'd ever wanted anything in her life, and she knew he wanted her just as much.

Their coming together had been fated, she thought, something neither of them could deny or prevent.

Bryce laid her on his bed, opening her robe so he could look at her while he undressed. Then he quickly stripped off his clothes.

Amy couldn't take her eyes off him. He was beautiful with his trim, athletic body and sculpted muscles. As her gaze traveled downward, she saw how much he wanted her. Her own body responded, and she knew she was wet and ready for him.

Amy would have imagined she'd be scared this first time with a man after the fiasco of her marriage to Cole. But she wasn't. Somehow she knew that no matter how much Bryce might desire her, he would never hurt her the way Cole had. Cole was a rough lover who thought nothing of pinching her or forcing her when she wasn't in the mood. But Bryce wasn't that kind of man, and Amy knew it.

Their lovemaking was everything she imagined it

would be…and more. Once Bryce was naked, he lay down beside her, and for the longest time, he caressed her and kissed her. Only after he'd brought her to the point where she was practically begging him to enter her did he finally raise up over her. Putting his hands under her buttocks, he pushed in. Amy gasped when she felt the tip of his penis deep inside.

She held him tight as they found their rhythm. And when, soon after, the first waves of pleasure shook her, followed by his own cries of release, she knew she hadn't been wrong. This man belonged with her. They belonged together. And somehow, some way, they would work out their problems.

It was only hours later, as Amy lay awake listening to Bryce's quiet breathing beside her, that she felt the first stirring of disquiet.

What would Bryce say when he found out she had been lying to him? Would he understand? Or would he feel betrayed?

She knew she had to come clean. And she would. Tomorrow, preferably. Over breakfast—for surely they'd eat breakfast together—she would tell him everything. And together they would figure out what to do next.

Chapter Eleven

It was still dark outside when Bryce awakened to the warmth of Amy's body curled beside him and the peaceful whisper of her lengthened breaths. He lay there for a long while, basking in contentment until he decided to get up and figure out what to fix the two of them for breakfast.

Too bad he didn't have some fresh cinnamon rolls. He'd scramble eggs to go with them, if he did. There was some bacon in the freezer, though. And he knew how to make waffles. He smiled, liking the idea of surprising her with something he'd made with his own hands.

He slipped out of bed quietly so as not to disturb

her. Even more quietly, he found clean briefs and a pair of jeans. Barefoot and bare-chested, he started to leave the bedroom. Then he stopped, looking over at the dresser where a framed photo of Michelle had sat ever since her death.

He stared at it for a long time, then walked over to pick it up. *I'll never forget you,* he told her smiling face, *but it's time to move on.* Her eyes seemed to be looking straight at him, and he felt she was telling him to be happy, just as he would have wanted her to find someone to love again if he'd been the one to die. With a pang of sadness, he quietly slid open the top drawer and placed the photo inside.

Before leaving the bedroom, he glanced at Amy again. Michelle would have approved, he thought, and wondered if it were just possible Michelle had sent Amy to him.

In the kitchen, as the coffee dripped, Bryce thought about last night and what had happened between him and Amy. He certainly hadn't intended to make love with her. In fact, he'd intended just the opposite. When he'd left El Paso, he'd made up his mind to come home and sit down and have a frank talk with Amy.

He'd been going to tell her that, yes, he was attracted to her, but he didn't think it would be a good idea for them to become involved. He'd told himself they were both adults and they could and would be sensible about the attraction between them, for Bryce had been certain Amy felt it, too.

How we fool ourselves.

Hell, he'd hardly been in the house two minutes when he was undressing her.

Not that he was sorry. He wasn't. Making love with Amy had been wonderful. Amy was wonderful. And despite what his mother thought, she was also eminently suitable to be his wife.

She was pretty and smart and sweet and she loved his children. Plus she was sensible, down to earth and honest. Someone he instinctively knew he could trust, not just with his children but with his heart. Those were qualities to cherish. They were also qualities that were hard to find. Again, despite his mother's preferences, he knew Tara was lacking some of them.

But this wasn't about Tara. Right now Amy was the only woman he wanted to think about.

He didn't plan to jump into anything, but he certainly wasn't interested in an affair. His intentions toward Amy were honorable, and he intended to tell her so.

And the sooner, the better, he thought with a smile.

He was in the middle of cooking waffles when the phone rang. He grabbed it on the first ring.

"Bryce." It was Jack Feegan.

Bryce expelled a frustrated sigh. "Jesus, Jack. *Now* what?"

''The men want to see something in writing about the four-day work week.''

''They don't *trust* me?'' Bryce couldn't believe it. Business at Hathaway had always been conducted on a handshake, and Bryce guessed he had thought it always would be.

''It's more they don't trust anybody right now. They're not stupid, Bryce. They hear the news stories. They read the paper. They see how many companies are reneging on their promises. Hell, some of them have fathers who have lost all kinds of retirement benefits they were counting on. It's a different world out there now.''

The anger Bryce had felt a moment ago evaporated. How could he blame the men? He'd been outraged himself when he'd read about companies who had adopted creative accounting to reward those at the top while taking away from those at the bottom. To be fair, the men were right to try to get some written guarantees. Of course, Bryce thought dryly, even written guarantees could be breached if a company had good enough lawyers.

''I know it's Saturday,'' Feegan continued, ''but do you think you could fax over something that I could show them?''

''Sure, no problem.'' Bryce hung up after promising to go into the office right away to take care of Jack's request.

He waited until the waffle in the waffle maker was

finished, then unplugged the appliance. After wrapping the waffle in foil, he walked back to the bedroom.

Amy was still sleeping. He watched her for a few seconds. She looked like a kid, with her petite body curled on its side. Her hands were tucked beneath her pillow, and her dark hair lay in a curly cascade, hiding half her face. But she sure wasn't a kid. She was all woman. Bryce smiled again. Definitely all woman, with a healthy sexual appetite to match his own.

Bryce didn't have the heart to wake her. He knew she rarely had a chance to sleep in. He decided he'd dress quietly, then write her a note and leave it for her on the kitchen table.

Ten minutes later he folded the note he'd written and put it right in the middle of the plate he'd put out earlier.

He was whistling as he left the compound.

Amy awakened with the sun shining on her face. She stretched luxuriously as memories of last night flooded her. Awareness of her surroundings gradually permeated her consciousness, and she rolled over, thinking Bryce was beside her.

When she saw that he wasn't, she sat up. The house seemed very quiet to her. She frowned, wondering where he was. It was Saturday, so he didn't have to go into work. He *did* often go into the office on Saturdays, but surely today he wouldn't, at least not before at least saying good morning.

He must be in the kitchen or in his office. Amy swung her legs out of bed and bent down to retrieve her robe, which lay in a jumble on the floor.

Her face heated as she remembered how she'd lost that robe. She closed her eyes, reliving those thrilling moments. Even thinking about what had happened between her and Bryce made her body tingle.

Feeling a bit like an interloper, she walked into Bryce's bathroom and splashed water on her face. Her hair needed brushing and so did her teeth. Maybe she'd better go on up to her own bathroom before looking for Bryce. That way she could put on some undies and lipstick. Maybe even a dab of perfume.

Humming to herself, she left the bedroom.

She had to pass Bryce's office to get to the stairs and couldn't help but see the door was open and he wasn't inside. So he must be in the kitchen. Probably drinking coffee and reading the morning paper.

But as she softly climbed the stairs, she didn't hear anything, not the rustle of pages, not the scrape of a chair, nothing.

Midway upstairs, she reversed course and came back down. Even before she reached the kitchen, she knew Bryce wasn't there, either.

Her gaze quickly took in the half-full coffeepot still warming, the table set for two, the waffle iron, and the note sitting in the middle of one of the plates.

Walking over, she picked it up. Her name was written on the outside.

Opening it, she read:

Amy, I'm really sorry, but I had to go into the office on something that couldn't wait. There's a waffle cooked and ready in the oven for you. I should be home by twelve.
Bryce

Disappointment mingled with a vague sense of bewilderment and hurt. The note was so impersonal. Exactly what he would have written before last night. There was nothing about how he felt, nothing about seeing her later, not even "Love, Bryce" at the end. Just "Bryce."

Amy crumpled the note in her fist.

He was sorry about what had happened between them. He was trying to tell her, with this cryptic, impersonal note, that she wasn't to get any ideas just because he'd taken her to his bed. He couldn't have been more clear if he'd written, "Sorry, babe, but last night was just a roll in the hay...nothing else."

Tears welled in her eyes as she berated herself for being stupid. *Stupid, stupid, stupid.* She couldn't believe it. After telling herself again and again what a mistake it would be to get involved with Bryce, that there could never be a happy ending if she did, she'd gone and done it, anyway!

You have got to be the dumbest, the most gullible, the silliest, the most naive woman in the world, and you deserve whatever happens next.

Amy trembled.

But Calista doesn't....

Now Amy's tears fell harder and she sank down onto a kitchen chair. Lowering her head onto her arms, she sobbed her heart out.

It took thirty minutes before her tears dried up. Furious with herself by now, she got up, poured herself a cup of coffee, turned off the coffeepot, then determinedly headed upstairs. She intended to shower and dress and be gone when Bryce returned. She would collect Calista, then maybe drive into Austin and do some shopping. She would not return until this evening. She would leave him a note the way he'd left her one, and hers would be even more impersonal.

I will not let him know that he's hurt me or that I expected anything from him. I may not have much else, but at least I'll have my pride.

An hour later she was on her way to Lorna's.

When Bryce's private line rang sometime around eleven-fifteen, he had just finished faxing the promised papers to Jack Feegan. He grabbed the phone immediately, thinking it was probably Amy. He was smiling when he said hello.

"Bryce? I was hoping to find you in the office.

I've been calling the house, but there was no answer.''

It wasn't Amy. It was Tara.

His smile faded. Now what?

"Bryce, I just got the morning's mail. In it there was one of those circulars. You know the kind. They say 'Have you seen us?' then they put pictures of missing persons on them?''

"Yes?"

"Well, on the one that came today, the pictures were of a woman and a little girl. Amy and Calista.''

"What?"

"I thought that would shock you.'' The tone of satisfaction in her voice was impossible to miss. "I *told* you there was something strange about her, but you wouldn't listen. Well, now the truth comes out. Under the pictures it says their names are Amy and Calista *Jordan,* and describes both exactly, so there's no mistake. It's them, all right. Seems your nanny stole her child from the father, who has custody. And she didn't live in Shreveport, either. She lived in Mobile.''

Until that moment Bryce thought some mistake had been made. It was just some wild coincidence that a woman named Amy and a child named Calista were missing. They couldn't be his Amy and her Calista. No way. But hearing Tara say Mobile told him there had been no mistake, because he vividly remembered the envelope he'd found in the trash.

The one that had contained the letter from Amy's father. The one with a return address in Mobile.

He also thought about how she hadn't taken him up on his suggestion to invite her father to visit. He thought about how she never made any phone calls or got any other letters. He thought about how she'd always turned the subject away from herself whenever possible and how she seemed to dislike answering questions.

All this time he'd believed she was just a very private person, one who didn't like to talk about herself. Now he knew why.

She was on the run.

She had taken her child illegally.

"Bryce? Are you still there?"

"I'm here," he said wearily, his mind whirling as he tried to think rationally.

"I've already called the 800 number on the circular. So you don't have to do anything. Boy, it's lucky I saw this, isn't it? The last thing you want is some fugitive watching the girls."

Bryce didn't even remember hanging up. For long minutes, he sat there staring into space. He couldn't believe it. Amy. A liar. A woman who had defied a court order and taken her child from her legal guardian.

Had anything she'd said and done been honest?

Had last night been honest?

The pain of her betrayal cut deeply. It was obvious

to him that she didn't feel the same way about him that he did about her. If she had, she would have trusted him enough to confide in him. The fact she hadn't told him volumes.

What a fool you are.

Okay, so he was a fool, but that didn't answer the big question. What should he do now?

Amy picked Calista up at ten, made a stop at the pharmacy, and then headed for the post office where she needed to buy some stamps. Her hurt feelings had calmed, and she was beginning to think maybe she'd overreacted to Bryce's note. Most men, especially men like Bryce, were cautious about expressing their feelings. They especially didn't like writing what they felt.

Still, she was glad this had happened, because maybe she should be cautious, too. This morning she'd been ready to blurt out everything, but maybe that would be a mistake. Maybe she should first let Bryce declare himself. If he said he loved her, and Amy hoped he did, then she could come clean. Until then she might be wise to keep her secret a secret.

Feeling better, she decided when she finished at the post office she would go back to the house so she'd be there at noon when Bryce came home. She knew they needed to talk.

She bought her stamps, said hello to a couple of people who greeted her, and was on her way out of the building when something on the ground near the doorway caught her eye.

It was a flyer.

One of those missing children flyers that came in the mail. Someone had discarded theirs and hadn't bothered to throw it into the trash bin.

Amy stared at it. At first her mind didn't register what she was seeing. When it did, she felt as if someone had struck her.

No, no, no, no.

Yet no matter how she denied it, the two pictures staring up at her were hers and Calista's.

Shaking, Amy bent down and picked up the flyer: "Missing since August 12th. Amy Jordan and Calista Jordan. Last seen in Mobile, Alabama."

Oh, God.

Her heart pounded so hard it scared her. She looked around furtively, sure every person in the place was watching her. But no one was even glancing her way. Almost sobbing now, Amy stuffed the flyer into her purse.

What am I going to do? she cried inside as she buckled Calista into her car seat. Even as she asked herself the question, she instinctively headed for Bryce's house, because down deep, she knew her only choice was to run. She didn't know when the flyer had hit local mailboxes, but she imagined it was this morning. Otherwise, surely someone would have noticed and said something. *Lorna* would have said something.

Amy swallowed, once more fighting tears. *Lorna.* Her friend had been so good to her. She would be so hurt that Amy hadn't trusted her enough to tell her the truth. Amy couldn't even think about Bryce. What he would think and feel she didn't know, but she could imagine. If he had entertained any ideas about making Amy a permanent part of his life, they'd be gone now.

He'll hate me.

It was nearly eleven when Amy pulled into the Hathaway compound and eleven-fifteen by the time she'd dragged out her bags and begun to load her and Calista's belongings into them. At eleven twenty-five, she lugged them downstairs. The whole time Calista kept asking bewildered questions, and Amy kept telling her, "It's okay, honey, it's okay."

"But where are we *going,* Mommy?" Calista cried.

Amy fought her own tears. Crying wouldn't do her a bit of good now. It was way too late for tears.

At eleven-thirty everything they owned was jammed into the trunk of Amy's car. Amy grabbed a couple of apples, a box of Cheerios, several juice boxes and several bottles of water, because she knew she could not stop. Not anytime soon.

Leaving the keys to the house along with the cell phone Bryce had given her on the kitchen table, she scribbled a fast note, saying only, "I'm sorry. Please forgive me. Amy."

At exactly eleven thirty-four she pulled out of the compound for the last time.

"Oh, no! Oh, poor Amy!"

Bryce was on his way home, but he'd called Lorna on his cell phone to ask her to meet him there. "Lorna, she lied to us."

"Yes, I know. But, Bryce, she wasn't lying when she told me about her ex. I know she wasn't. You could see the truth in her eyes."

Yeah, Bryce thought, *that's what I thought last night. But I was wrong.* "Maybe she's just a damned good liar. Did you ever think of that?"

"Bryce! You don't believe that."

"Don't I?"

"You're obviously just upset."

"I have a reason to be upset. This is a woman who hasn't told us the truth about anything, and I entrusted my children to her." *Not to mention my heart.*

"I know, I know, but come on, Bryce. Amy was probably scared to death that her ex would find her. I'm sure she felt she had no choice but to keep the truth from us. C'mon, Bryce, bend a little. If she's seen the flyer she's probably frantic. We have to help her!"

"We're wasting time talking, Lorna."

"All right. I'm on my way."

Bryce wondered what Lorna would say when she found out Tara had already notified the authorities of Amy's whereabouts.

Amy had no idea where she was going, but she figured she might as well head in the same direction she'd been heading when she first saw the sign for Morgan Creek.

She wanted to wail. She wanted to scream. She wanted to beat her fists against the steering wheel and rant against the gods. She could do none of these things. Because what *she* wanted and the way *she* felt wasn't important.

You forgot that. But don't forget it again. Calista is the one who counts. The only one.

Bryce found the note within minutes of entering the house. Even before he found it, he knew Amy was gone. He could feel the emptiness in the air. When she was there, the house felt warm and welcoming.

Now it felt cold and lonely.

Amy, why? Why couldn't you trust me?

Lorna arrived a few minutes later.

"She's gone," he said.

"Gone? Where?"

Bryce shrugged.

"Are you sure? Maybe she's still out running errands. She said she had a few things to do when she picked up Calista. Have you checked her room?''

Hope flared. Maybe she *wasn't* gone. Maybe it was like Lorna said. Maybe she was just out, running errands, in which case they'd better find her before the authorities did. Then he saw the keys. ''We can check her room, but she's gone. She left her keys.''

''Oh, no. Poor Amy. Do you think she saw the flyer?''

''She must have. Why else would she leave?'' For a moment he felt guilty and wondered if there was any chance what had happened between them last night had had something to do with her flight. But that was crazy. Why would it?

''Let's go upstairs and just make sure,'' Lorna said.

Bryce felt sorry for her. She was grasping at straws.

''Tara called that 800 number listed on the flyer,'' Bryce said as he and Lorna climbed the stairs and headed toward Amy's rooms.

''Bitch.''

Bryce bit back a smile.

''I can just see the look on her face when she did it, too,'' Lorna said. ''You know, Bryce, if you should *ever* entertain the notion of starting up with Tara again, I will personally pull your fingernails out one by one.''

He couldn't help laughing, although it did nothing

to ease the pain in his gut at the sight of the empty closet and dresser drawers.

"She can't be gone long," Lorna said. "I mean, she didn't even pick Calista up until ten. And it would have taken time to come home and pack."

Bryce looked at his watch. It was exactly eleven fifty-five. He figured at best Amy had maybe a thirty-minute lead. And there were only two roads out of Morgan Creek.

"We have to help her, Bryce. If the police find her, she's toast."

He nodded. She was right. "You take Hathaway Road," he said, naming the road that passed by their main plant, "and I'll take Trent Road. Maybe we can catch her before anyone else does."

Bryce drove too fast. The anger and betrayal he'd felt earlier was still there, but superceding those emotions was a sense of urgency and the sure knowledge that he had to find Amy before the authorities did.

No matter what she'd done or how many lies she'd told him and his family, he didn't want to see her tossed into jail. For Calista's sake alone, he knew he had to do something to help. At the very least he wanted to hear Amy's side of the story.

When he reached the highway that led to San Marcos in one direction and Interstate 10 and points east in the other direction, he debated, but only for a few seconds. She would not take I-10. She would avoid main roads because that's where the authorities would look first.

He turned west, in the direction of San Marcos.

Cole slapped his desk in triumph.

They'd found her! In Texas. In some Podunk town called Morgan Creek. What the hell she was doing there, he couldn't imagine, but the woman who had called the hotline number had been positive. She was working there as a nanny for a family named Hathaway. She hadn't even bothered to change their names. Cole grinned. He'd always known Amy wasn't the brightest star in the sky, and this sure proved it. Sure, she'd escaped him for a while, but that was due to luck, not brains.

But he had her now.

And this time she wouldn't get away.

Chapter Twelve

As the miles lengthened between her and Morgan Creek, Amy's spirits plummeted in direct proportion to the distance.

If only she'd had time to say goodbye to Lorna and Bryce. If only she could have explained. If only she thought she'd see them again someday.

Her whole life was a series of "if onlys," she thought in despair. *Must I keep on paying because I made one mistake?* But that mistake had given her Calista, a fact she could never regret.

Stop feeling sorry for yourself. You knew it was foolhardy to get involved with Bryce. And you knew Cole might eventually trace your whereabouts. Now get over it and focus on what you're going to do now.

What *was* she going to do?

Maybe she would be wise to head south. Go into Mexico and lose herself there. But at the thought, Amy's spirts dropped even farther. Her knowledge of Spanish was minimal, her resources limited. What kind of job could she get in Mexico? And what would she do when her money ran out?

No. Mexico wasn't an option. She would have to stay in the U.S. or else go north to Canada. She would also have to try to disguise herself, something she had hoped would not be necessary. Maybe color her hair red or blond and cut it short. Buy some glasses to wear or maybe even colored contact lenses. Amy wondered if she was going to have to change their names. But that would mean contacting the network again, seeing if there was someplace similar in California where she might be able to get new documentation.

With new papers, she'd be able to look for another job. And they'd need a place to live. Just the thought of everything ahead of her made her feel sick to her stomach. She was so scared and so heartsick over having to leave Morgan Creek and the people she had come to love.

Oh, Bryce.

Even the thought of what had happened between them less than twelve hours earlier made her eyes swim with unshed tears. How could she survive knowing she would never again feel the comfort of his arms or the ecstasy of his kisses?

Realizing Calista was no longer crying, Amy looked back and saw that her baby had fallen asleep. Thank God. Amy wasn't sure she could have stood watching Calista cry any longer.

Amy no longer tried to stop her own tears. Since Calista wasn't awake to see them, she could finally give in to the misery that permeated her every cell.

What had Bryce thought when he read her note? What was he thinking now? Amy could only imagine.

And the girls.

Oh, God, the girls. Susan and Stella. How would they feel when they returned tomorrow and found that Amy and Calista were gone? For them, it would be another loss, another desertion.

Oh, Amy, Amy, she berated herself, *you are hurting so many people.*

But what else could she have done?

She was in this lowest possible frame of mind when she happened to glance in the rearview mirror to see a black Mercedes bearing down on her. Her heart slammed against her chest.

Bryce!

It had to be Bryce!

He'd somehow figured out which direction she'd

gone, and now he was coming after her. Dear heaven. What should she do?

And yet, even as she asked herself the question, she knew the answer. Her Toyota couldn't outrun Bryce's more powerful car. Plus she would never jeopardize her daughter's life by driving recklessly. She really had no choice except to stop.

Scared and sick at heart, she slowed and pulled to the side of the road.

Bryce felt an overwhelming surge of relief when he spotted Amy's car. And he was very glad she showed enough sense to pull over. If he'd had to chase her, he might have been forced to call the police rather than take a chance on endangering her and Calista.

He pulled in behind her, then got out of his car and walked over to hers. She'd already lowered her driver's-side window. She didn't say anything, just looked up at him with those big eyes of hers.

He could see she'd been crying. Her eyes and nose were all red and swollen. He could also see how frightened she was. It was painful to witness her misery and fear, even as he was filled with disappointment that she'd felt the need to run from him.

Amy, why couldn't you have trusted me?

For a long moment they just looked at each other. Then they both spoke at once.

"I'm glad I found—" Bryce began.

"I'm sorry I didn't—" she said. Then she took a deep, shuddering breath. Her voice wobbled when she continued. "I...I'm so sorry, Bryce. I know you must hate me."

"Oh, Amy," he answered wearily, "I don't hate you. I'm just disappointed that you think so little of me that you felt you had to run away again. That you didn't trust me enough to tell me the truth."

Her eyes swam with tears.

"I want you to turn around and come back to the house."

"I can't!"

"Amy, think. You can't keep running. Sooner or later you'll be caught, and then what? You'll go to jail. Do you want that?" He looked pointedly at Calista, who was sleeping in her car seat and hadn't stirred.

"No!" she cried. "Of course, I don't want that. But you don't understand. I can't let Calista go back to Cole, either. He's...he's a terrible person, Bryce. He doesn't love her."

Bryce wanted to ask why he'd been given custody of their daughter if he was so terrible, but this was no place to talk. "I'd like to understand, and if you come back to the house where we can talk quietly, I promise I'll try to help you."

"No one can help."

"Why don't you let me be the judge of that?"

She lowered her head. "I'm so tired of being afraid," she whispered.

"Then come back with me. Tell me everything, and maybe I can figure out a way to help."

It took her a while, but she finally said she would. Bryce waited until she'd turned her car around, then followed her back to the compound. On the way, Bryce called Lorna on her cell phone and told her to meet them there.

When they got to the house, Amy took Calista upstairs to bed. Exhausted from her crying, the child still hadn't awakened. By the time Amy came downstairs again, Bryce had put a pot of coffee on.

"I've called Lorna and asked her to join us."

Amy nodded. She looked utterly spent.

"I'd like you to tell me everything from the beginning," he said, "but maybe you'd like to wait until Lorna gets here."

She nodded again.

"Amy..."

Her eyes met his.

Bryce shook his head. "Never mind." There were a million things he wanted to say, but he knew it would be best to wait until she'd had a chance to explain herself.

They didn't have long to wait. Ten minutes later Lorna walked in the back door. She walked straight over to Amy and bent down to hug her. As Bryce watched them he couldn't help remembering how it had felt to hold Amy last night and how happy he'd been.

Ruthlessly he pushed the memory away. Last night he'd been living in a fool's paradise. Today he'd been rudely thrust back into the real world.

Bryce didn't intend to make the same mistake twice.

"I can't explain what happened unless I start from the beginning," Amy said. She kept her gaze trained on Lorna, because she couldn't stand to see the look of disappointment in Bryce's eyes.

"Just tell us in your own way," Lorna said kindly.

Bryce said nothing.

Amy took a deep breath. "When I graduated from college, I couldn't find a teaching position in Fort Myers, so through a connection of a sorority sister of mine, I was hired to teach kindergarten at one of the top schools in Mobile." Remembering how happy she'd been during her two years there, Amy smiled. "It was a good time for me. I loved the school and I loved teaching.

"I became friendly with one of the other teachers and one day she invited me to attend a fund-raiser for a local charity with her and her husband. Cole, that's my ex, was there and her husband knew him and introduced us. Cole was charming and very attentive and when he asked me out, I was flattered. Over the next weeks, he bombarded me with attention. He sent me flowers, he took me to wonderful restaurants and concerts, he bought me expensive presents. It was overwhelming. I...I was no match for him. I was barely twenty-four and pretty unsophisticated, and he knew it. He played me perfectly. Before I knew what had happened, we were engaged. We were married less than five months after we'd met.''

Lorna made a sympathetic sound. Amy chanced a quick look at Bryce. His expression was unreadable.

Trying to keep her voice impersonal and unemotional, Amy continued. ''Cole was an assistant district attorney at the time, a very smart, very persuasive man. I looked up to him. He didn't want me to work, even though I felt differently. I gave in, especially when he said it was important to him to have a wife who could devote all her time to him. He wanted to run for political office, and he said I'd be a great help to him, that we'd be a team.

''At first everything was great. I loved being a wife, and I loved taking care of our home. And I loved feeling important to Cole. I couldn't even tell you when things began to change. At first, the changes were subtle. I hardly noticed how he gradually distanced me from my friends or how he discouraged me from doing anything that didn't include him. Then one day I realized that I had no life of my own, that I wasn't even picking out my own clothes anymore.

"I still wasn't alarmed. I realized Cole had a very strong and dominant personality and was a bit of a control freak. I decided it would be good for me *and* for him if I were to assert myself more and try to be more independent. I figured Cole would soon realize it was more interesting to have a wife who had some ideas of her own than one who followed him like a lamb."

"And that's when the trouble started," Lorna said.

Amy grimaced. "Yes. I'll never forget the first time I defied him. We were going to a party, one where Cole hoped to rally some backers, and he told me to wear this black dress that he liked. I didn't like it because it was too low cut and it made me feel uncomfortable, so I put on something else. Cole didn't see me beforehand because we were meeting at the party, and when he *did* see me, he was furious. He was so angry he left red marks on my arm where he squeezed it too hard. And that night..." She took a deep breath. "He hurt me that night."

"He *hit* you?" Bryce said.

"No, but he..." Amy couldn't look at Bryce. She didn't want to talk about specifics. She was too ashamed that she'd allowed Cole to treat her the way he had.

"You don't have to explain," Lorna said. "I get the picture."

"Things seemed to get worse and worse after that," Amy said. "He insisted on making every decision, and if I disagreed with him, he'd ridicule me. He put me down every chance he got. One time I corrected him in front of some of his friends. It wasn't anything big, just something he said that was wrong, and I corrected him. Oh, God. I'll never forget that. He gave me the ugliest look, then made a horrible, insulting remark. And that night…'' She shuddered. ''Then the next day he gave me the silent treatment. That lasted more than a week.''

''Why didn't you leave him?''

Amy finally met Bryce's gaze. ''I can't explain it to you. I kept thinking I was doing something wrong. That if only I could find the way to be the kind of wife Cole needed, everything would be okay. I know how stupid that sounds, but at the time, I really believed I was at fault.''

''I understand,'' Lorna said. She reached over and clasped Amy's hand. ''Women have a tendency to blame themselves when things don't go right. We always think it's our responsibility to keep our worlds working the way they should.''

Amy smiled at her. What a wonderful friend Lorna was. ''After that, I pretty much just went along with anything and everything Cole said, and for a while things were much better.'' She sighed.

''Then I got pregnant. Cole was livid when I told him. He called me a stupid bitch. He said I couldn't get even the simplest things right. I was stunned. I'd actually thought Cole would be happy I was going to have his child. It was only later that I realized why he wasn't happy. A child would take up too much of my time.

"But I'm getting ahead of myself. I kept thinking that once our baby was born, Cole would change his mind. He would love the baby, and everything would be the way I knew it could be." She smiled wryly. "I was so wrong. Things actually were much worse after Calista was born. For one thing, Cole *didn't* love her. I really think he's incapable of loving her, of loving anyone. Cole *possesses* people and only insofar as they're valuable to him.

"When Calista was a year old, I knew, for her sake if not mine, I had to leave him, but I was really scared. I just didn't know what he'd do. Finally, three months before Calista's second birthday, I worked up enough courage to actually go through with it. I packed up our things, hers and mine, and I left. I went to Florida, to my father's house, and then I filed for divorce."

Amy spoke rapidly now, just wanting to get this over with. She finished by telling them how Cole had fought her. How he'd filed a countersuit saying she'd deserted him. How'd he'd gotten people to lie for him. To say Amy wasn't fit to raise Calista. How they'd seen her doing drugs and how she neglected her daughter. She described what it was like to lose custody of Calista. How it broke her heart to only be able to see her baby twice a week and then only under supervision. She told how she found out about the underground network through an Internet support group. How she'd planned and waited and finally found her opportunity to take Calista.

"Did you plan to come to Morgan Creek?" Lorna asked.

"No. It was a fluke that I saw the sign. But the moment I did, I thought of you. All I really wanted when I came was a safe place to stay overnight. I never dreamed I'd be offered a job." Her gaze met Bryce's. "When you asked me if I was interested in becoming your daughters' nanny, I really felt God was watching out for me, because the position seemed heaven sent. I…I…" Her voice faltered. She swallowed, then took a deep breath. She must keep her emotions under control. "I just want you to know that I have loved working for you. The only…lies I told you had to do with my past. Not with the present." *Please,* she prayed. *Please forgive me.*

"Can you give me a list of the people who testified against you?" Bryce asked.

Amy was taken aback. Whatever she'd been expecting him to say, it wasn't that. "Yes."

"You're going to help her, aren't you?" Lorna said. She smiled at her brother.

"If she can give me the names of the witnesses, I'll have our law firm get an investigator to check them out. Based on what they find, I'll see if there's anything that can be done."

Amy fought to keep from bursting into tears, she was so grateful. "So you believe me?" she finally managed.

Bryce nodded.

"Thank you."

"You can't stay here, though." Before she could respond, he said, "Tara saw the flyer and she called that 800 number. So by now I'm sure your ex knows where you are. From the way you described him, I'd bet he's on his way. And if the police are involved, there's no way I can keep him off the compound."

The fear that had abated when Amy realized Bryce was going to help her now returned in full force.

"Don't worry, hon," Lorna said, "we'll find a safe place for you."

Bryce thought for a few minutes. "Lorna, why don't you take Amy and Calista into Austin? I know Chloe will put them up. You can hide Amy's car in your garage and go in yours."

"That's perfect. No one would think to look for you there," Lorna said.

"In fact, I think you should stay at Chloe's, too. That way you won't have to answer any questions or tell any lies if the authorities come sniffing around."

"But what about work?" Lorna said.

"I'll just tell people you've taken the week as vacation."

"Okay. I'll go call Chloe right now."

''Bryce,'' Amy said, ''what will you tell Susan and Stella?''

''I don't know. Maybe that you had a family emergency?''

Amy nodded slowly. ''Wh-what will you do for someone to watch them?''

''They'll have to stay at my parents' house after school until I can find someone to take your place.''

His words hit Amy hard. They seemed so final. As if there was no possibility of her coming back. *But you knew that, didn't you?*

After that, Amy didn't have an opportunity to talk to Bryce again. She wondered if he'd purposely made sure that was the case. While Lorna called Chloe—who was happy to help them out—he disappeared into his office and closed the door. When she got off the phone, she called him, and the three of them transferred all of Amy's and Calista's belongings into Lorna's SUV. Only then did Amy wake Calista.

''Be careful,'' Bryce said to Lorna. ''Call when you get there.''

''All right.''

He finally turned to Amy. ''Good luck. I'll be in touch.''

Amy searched his eyes for a spark of tenderness, but there was nothing. It was as if he'd closed himself off from any emotion.

What did you expect, Amy? She had to force herself not to look back when they pulled out of his driveway.

It took nearly forty minutes to get to Lorna's, put Amy's car in her garage and for Lorna to pack up enough to last her the week. Finally they were on their way. For a long time they said nothing, each lost in her own thoughts. Calista hummed happily in the backseat, excited about her "venture," which Lorna had touted.

When Lorna spoke, her voice was soft and reassuring. "It's going to be all right, Amy."

But Lorna didn't know the whole story. Yes, Amy now had hope that Bryce would be able to perform a miracle for her and she would be able to keep Calista, but she had no hope whatsoever that things could ever work out between her and Bryce.

"When you've got plenty of money and the right connections," Lorna continued, misconstruing Amy's silence for doubt, "you can do just about anything. And Bryce has both."

"I'll never be able to repay either of you for all you've done for me," Amy said.

After that, they fell silent. Amy looked out of the window and tried not to think about anything. Lorna fiddled with the radio until she found a station she liked.

Just before they reached the Austin city limits, Lorna lowered the volume of the radio and said, "Amy, if things work out for you and you get custody of Calista, will you come back to Morgan Creek and continue working for Bryce?''

Amy chose her words carefully. She knew Lorna didn't suspect what had happened between her and Bryce, and she had no intention of telling her. It wouldn't be fair to Lorna, because then she'd be torn between her friendship with Amy and her loyalty to her brother. ''I think that would be up to Bryce. Don't you?''

The next morning Bryce was barely out of bed when he got a call from the front gate. It was Deputy Sheriff Tim Reilly, a highschool classmate of Claudia's.

''Hey, Bryce. I need to come in and talk to you. You got a few minutes?''

''Sure, Tim. I'll open the gate for you.'' Bryce released the lock, then hurriedly brushed his teeth and hair and walked out to the kitchen to plug in the coffeemaker. A minute later the front doorbell rang.

When Bryce opened the door, he wasn't surprised to see Tim had brought someone with him. The other man was shorter than Tim, probably just a bit shy of six feet, and darker, with almost a Mediterranean look about him. He had thick black hair and dark, shrewd eyes. The clothes he wore were designer brands, beautifully tailored. Bryce knew without being told that this was Cole Jordan.

Tim introduced them, and Bryce invited the two

men in. Although he would have liked nothing better than to punch Cole Jordan's lights out, he was very polite.

"We've got a court order to detain the woman calling herself Amy Gordon," Tim said. "Her real name's Amy Jordan, and she took Mr. Jordan's daughter illegally."

"I'm afraid you made a trip for nothing. She's not here."

"Now c'mon, Bryce," Tim said. "Mr. Jordan here has the law on his side, so you're not doing her any good by hiding her."

"I'm not hiding her. She left yesterday, very suddenly."

"She must have said something," Tim said.

"I wasn't here when she left." Bryce was surprised at how easy it was to lie.

"Somebody must have warned her." This came from Jordan. He gave Bryce a hard stare.

Bryce stared back.

"So you don't know anything," Tim said.

"Just what I told you."

"Well, if you hear from her, I'd appreciate it if you'd call me," Tim said.

Bryce nodded.

Tim turned to Cole Jordan. "We'll put out an APB on her. Bryce, did you happen to notice what kind of plates she had on her car?"

"They were Florida plates," Bryce said smoothly.

He was getting pretty good at lying, he thought wryly.

"I don't suppose you know the license number."

"Sorry, no."

"I thought she was working for you as your nanny," Jordan snapped. "Didn't you think it might be smart to check up on her? Or do you just accept anyone who walks in your door at face value? To watch your children?"

Now it was Bryce's turn to give Jordan a hard look. "Not that it's any of your business who I employ or what I require of them," he said levelly, "but she had impeccable references."

Jordan flushed. "It *is* my business when my ex-wife, who was proven in court to be an unfit mother, takes off with my kid. And if you're not telling the truth, you're aiding and abetting a criminal, which is a felony."

"I believe it's also a felony to bribe witnesses to lie in court."

"Why you son of a bitch!" Jordan exploded. "You *do* know where she is, don't you? I'll bet you helped her get away."

Bryce knew he should never have made that crack about bribing witnesses, but he couldn't stand Cole Jordan, and he hadn't been able to resist baiting him. Ignoring Jordan's outburst, he said to Tim, "I've told you everything I know, Tim. Now if you don't mind, it's Sunday morning, and I haven't even had my coffee yet.'' Bryce rarely pulled rank in Morgan Creek, but he knew that Tim knew that Hathaway Bakery employed half the town and that all Bryce had to do was make one phone call and Tim would be out of a job.

"Sure, okay, Bryce, we'll be going. Sorry to have bothered you.''

Cole Jordan was seething, and Bryce knew he wanted to say a lot more, but he must have thought better of it because when Tim got up, he did, too.

Bryce watched as the two men got back into Tim's cruiser. Good riddance, he thought.

If he'd had any doubts at all about the truth of what Amy had told him, meeting Cole Jordan would have dispelled them. Although he'd wanted to help her before, now Bryce was determined that if it were the last thing he ever did, he would make sure Cole Jordan got what was coming to him for what he had done to Amy.

Chapter Thirteen

"Three of the five witnesses who testified against Mrs. Jordan in the custody hearing have admitted they were coerced into giving false information."

Bryce hadn't doubted Amy's story, but it was still nice to have corroboration. "What about the other two?" Bryce was talking to Lucas McConn, the investigator hired by the company's law firm.

"One's working in Germany. So far I haven't been able to contact him. The other one refused to talk to us. But I don't think you need those two. Not with the sworn statements from the three who recanted."

"Do those three understand they'll probably be called to appear in court?"

"Yes."

"And they're willing?"

"Let's put it this way," McConn said. "They know they don't have a choice."

"Did you make it clear they could go to jail for admitting they lied under oath?"

"Yeah."

"And they're *still* willing?"

"Thing is, I told them when the judge hears *why* they said what they did, I think he'll go easy on 'em. That Jordan is a real SOB. One of the women testified because he threatened to fire her if she didn't. Seems he'd written her up a couple of times for missing work, so he might have been able to terminate her without repercussions, even though the reason she had to miss so much work was because she's got this terminally ill kid. She's a single mother and said she couldn't take a chance on losing her job and her paid health insurance."

"But we can't be sure the judge will go easy on them. I'd hate to be responsible for someone like her going to jail and leaving her child."

"Her kid died two months ago. I think she feels she has nothing more to lose."

Bryce made a note to look into the woman's current financial situation and to do something for her. "What about the other two? Did they say why they lied?"

"They were scared silly, too, for other reasons.

One's a gay man, and he was still in the closet. Jordan had threatened to expose him. The other one had a kid in trouble for stealing a car, and Jordan said he'd make sure the charges were reduced. They all figured they *had* to do what he wanted, 'cause there was too much at stake. Plus they all thought nobody'd believe 'em if they reported him or tried to cross him, anyway.''

Bryce's jaw clenched. He had known men like Cole Jordan all of his life. Men who thought they were above the rules that governed everyone else. Men who felt a sense of entitlement and could justify every action in their own minds no matter how much that action might hurt another person. Hell, Jake Kenyon was a lot like that. So, come to think of it, was Tara. How Bryce had ever entertained the idea of marrying her, he didn't know.

Bryce wondered if he'd hear from Tara again. He knew she must have heard about Amy being gone. Knowing Tara, she would think the fact Amy had proven to be someone other than they'd believed would wipe out anything Tara might have done or said. He hadn't decided what he would say to her if she did call. He did know he was tired of scenes.

Which reminded him of the encounter he'd had with his mother the evening before. Kathleen had come storming over within minutes of Bryce getting home from the office. She'd just heard about Amy and demanded to know if he'd had anything to do with Amy's disappearance. "You'd better not be helping her evade the police, Bryce," she'd warned. "That would be really stupid."

Although Bryce always tried to be respectful of his mother, he wasn't about to be browbeaten by her and he'd let her know it.

They'd parted in anger. Now Bryce wondered how long it would be before he heard from his grandmother.

"Do you want me to overnight copies of my report and these affidavits to you?"

McConn's question snapped Bryce back to the present. "Yes. Send the originals to Levy along with your bill."

"Will do."

As soon as they hung up, Bryce called Chloe's house. He spoke first with Chloe, then asked to speak with Amy.

"Hello, Bryce." She sounded tired.

Bryce fought against feeling sorry for her. He couldn't afford any weakening—not until he decided what, if anything, the future held for them. "I've got some good news for you." He went on to explain what the investigator had uncovered. "With this information, I think the charges against you will be dropped and you'll be granted a new custody hearing."

"Oh, God, I hope you're right. When will we know?"

"I'm going to have my law firm send someone to Mobile tomorrow. As soon as I hear anything from him, I'll call."

"What will he do there?"

"The first thing will be to see if there's a warrant for your arrest. If there is, he'll talk to the D.A. and show him the evidence we have against your ex and try to get the charges against you dropped. If he can't, you'll have to appear in court. Don't worry, though. Our lawyer will explain everything to you. And he'll be with you all the way."

"Bryce, I am so thankful. I won't ever be able to repay you for this."

"Put that out of your mind. No repayment is necessary. Let's focus on getting this situation straightened out." *And getting that ex-husband of yours behind bars where he belongs.*

"All right."

"Now could you put Lorna on?"

"Oh. Of course. Th-thank you again."

"You're welcome." He knew she wanted something else from him. He could hear the need in her voice. But right now he was incapable of providing it, because he wasn't sure what he felt for her anymore. He'd thought he knew, but the bottom line was, Amy wasn't the person he'd believed her to be. No matter what the reason, she'd lied to him, and now he didn't know if he could ever trust her again.

Until he figured it out, it was best to keep their conversations matter-of-fact.

When Lorna came on the line, Bryce told her he thought she should accompany Amy and Calista to Mobile.

"But you'll be going, too, won't you?"

"I'm not sure."

Lorna was silent for a few seconds. When she did speak, she'd lowered her voice. "Bryce, is there something wrong between you and Amy?"

"What do you mean?"

"Don't play dumb. You've been acting weird, and she's been acting weird. Are you still upset about the fact she lied to us?"

"Don't you think I should be?"

"Will you stop answering my questions with another question?"

Now it was his turn to hesitate. "Look, Lorna, I know you mean well, but this is really between me and Amy."

"Just tell me one thing, Bryce. When all of this mess is straightened out…*if* it's straightened out…do you want Amy back?"

Again Bryce hesitated. "The truth is, I don't know."

"Oh, Bryce," she said sadly.

"I'm sorry. I just…don't know."

"I know you're right. This really isn't any of my business—"

"That's not what I said."

"It's what you meant, though. And that's okay. However, I'm going to say one last thing, then I'm hanging up. If you let Amy go, you're a fool. Yes, I know she lied to us, but she had a damned good reason. Here's what I want you to think about, Bryce. What if it were Susan and Stella that were in danger? Wouldn't you lie, too, to keep them safe?"

Two days later Bryce called again. Amy said a silent prayer before coming to the phone.

"Good news," he said without preamble. "The D.A. in Mobile has dropped the charges against you providing you bring Calista back to the Alabama court's jurisdiction immediately and appear before the family court judge for a new hearing."

Amy's eyes filled with tears. "Oh, Bryce, thank you." She was so relieved she was shaking.

"I've had my secretary make reservations for you, Calista and Lorna to fly to Mobile this afternoon. Josh Levy will meet you at the airport. He's the attorney who's been working on your behalf."

Amy wished Bryce was there in person instead of telling her all this on the phone. If only she could see his face. See if there was even a spark of tenderness in his expression. If only he were standing there in front of her. She would throw her arms around him to thank him, and maybe…just maybe…that horrible, impersonal tone of voice would disappear.

She didn't understand how he could have just wiped out what had happened between them. She knew she would never forget the night they spent together. And it wasn't just the sex that was unforgettable. It was Bryce's tenderness, the loving way he'd treated her, the look in his eyes. Being with her had meant something to him, something more than sexual desire fulfilled. But now whatever had been there seemed to have gone up in smoke, just as if it had never existed. This, more than anything, hurt her, for she knew she could never wipe out her feelings for him. They would haunt her for the rest of her life.

"By this time next week," Bryce was saying now, "your nightmare should be over."

"Do you really think I'll get custody of Calista?"

"Well, no judge is going to let Cole keep custody, that's for sure. In fact, I'd be willing to bet Cole will be arrested before the day is out."

"He *will?*"

"What he did is a felony, Amy. And as a former officer of the court himself, he knew better than most what he was doing was against the law."

Amy could hardly take it in. In her wildest dreams she'd never imagined Cole would be punished. Somehow Cole had always seemed invincible. But Bryce had taken him down. If only she believed

Bryce had done it out of love for her, she would be the happiest woman on earth.

"Let me talk to Lorna now," Bryce said. "And good luck in Mobile."

"You..." Amy swallowed. "You aren't coming?"

"You don't need me. Josh Levy knows exactly what to do, and Lorna will be there to lend moral support."

But I do need you, Amy cried silently. *I need you so badly.* Aloud she tried to keep her voice unemotional. "I guess this is goodbye, then."

"Take care, Amy. And don't worry. Everything's going to be fine."

She noticed he didn't say everything would be fine *between them,* and she knew it wasn't an idle omission. Pain engulfed her as the last, faint hope that Bryce would relent and forgive her faded. "Thank you," she whispered. Then she quietly put the phone down and went in search of Lorna.

Six Months Later

Missing Bryce was like having a sore that wouldn't heal. Sometimes it hurt more than other times, but it never disappeared entirely. And if you bumped it! Oh, God, the pain if you bumped it was indescribable.

Yet Amy had found she was stronger than she'd

imagined. She kept busy, and she tried not to dwell on what might have been but instead worked to concentrate on the future and what she might make of it.

Today was her last day of court-ordered community service—her only punishment for having broken the law in taking Calista. In many ways, she was sad to be saying goodbye to the people at Holy Spirit Ministry. In fact, she'd pretty much decided that if she remained in Mobile—something she was considering since her old school had offered her her job back in the fall—she would continue to volunteer at the ministry on Saturdays, as long as she could bring Calista along with her. The ministry provided day care for its volunteers' preschool-age children, so Calista was never far from Amy's sight.

Amy had now served the ministry in every capacity. She'd worked behind the scenes at Twice Blessed, the store where donated clothing, household goods, books and furniture were sold to raise money to operate the ministry. She'd worked in the food pantry, both stocking shelves and filling food orders for people in need. And lately she'd been helping out as a counselor in the financial assistance part of the center. She'd found the last job to be the most fascinating and rewarding of all. Hearing the stories of the people who came for help was a revelation to her. She'd had no idea there were so many people in need. Many of them had jobs, but their jobs paid so little, they simply couldn't manage to live on their income.

Others had suffered some disaster. An accident that wasn't covered by Workman's Compensation. A medical emergency and no health insurance. The death of a spouse, a divorce or an abandonment by the father of their children. So many sad stories.

Amy found that people liked talking to her. They seemed to sense that she, too, had suffered some serious problems and that she understood. She truly felt she'd gotten more from the work she'd done at the ministry than she'd contributed. Every day when she left with Calista to go home to her small apartment, she counted her blessings. Yes, she'd lost Bryce— there was that ache again—but she still had so much. A beautiful daughter who was doing so well, even though she still occasionally talked about Susan and Stella. Wonderful friends, including Lorna, who called several times a week and who had come to Mobile twice now in the past six months. A father who adored both her and her child and whom she adored back. And now, a good job offer once more. She was truly a fortunate woman.

So even though she would miss her daily work at the ministry, it was time for her to move on. To decide what she was going to do with the rest of her life.

As Amy drove home on a gorgeous day in late March, she decided that tonight she and Calista would splurge and go out to dinner. There was a small family-owned Italian restaurant only two blocks from Amy's apartment. They had a great children's menu and wonderful pasta. Yes, she thought, smiling, she deserved to celebrate tonight.

She was still smiling as she pulled up in front of the small complex where she lived. Normally she parked in back, under a covered slot, but since she planned to go out again fairly soon, she would just leave her car on the street. It wasn't until she was removing Calista from her car seat that she saw the car parked across the street.

It was a black Mercedes.

Her heart leaped crazily, even as she told herself not to get excited. There must be thousands of black Mercedes in the world.

And then, in a moment that she knew she would remember vividly the rest of her life, the driver's-side door opened and a tall man stepped out.

The sunlight blinded Amy, and it was a few seconds before her mind registered the astounding fact that the man was Bryce.

Stunned, Amy stood there holding Calista. She was incapable of moving. Incapable of forming a coherent thought.

Bryce.

He walked slowly across the street. He looked wonderful. He wore casual dark slacks and an open-necked dark shirt. His light-brown hair shone in the sunlight. Dark glasses concealed his eyes.

As feeling began to replace the numbness the first sight of him had caused, Amy's mind whirled. What was he doing there? Why had he come?

She was afraid to hope.

Her heart picked up speed as he reached her side of the street. He stopped a couple of feet away. "Hello, Amy."

"Bryce," she managed. She wet her lips. "I...I'm surprised to see you." She wished he wasn't wearing those glasses so she could see his eyes.

As if he'd heard her unspoken thought, he removed the glasses and hung them from the neck of his shirt. He looked at Calista and smiled. "Hi, Calista."

Calista was going through a shy period, and she hung her head and peeped up at him through her lashes. Amy shrugged. "Bashful," she explained.

Somehow, that broke the ice.

He nodded, the smile warm in his eyes. "Stella was like that at that age, too."

Now Amy smiled, too. "I finished my community service today." She couldn't believe how calm she sounded, when inside she was a whirlwind of emotions.

"Yes, I know. Lorna told me."

For long seconds their gazes held. Afterward Amy would never be sure who moved first. All she knew was the next moment, she and Calista both were wrapped in his embrace. He buried his face in her hair. "I love you, Amy," he murmured. "I've missed you like the devil."

Joy exploded at his words. "Oh, Bryce. I...I love you, too."

He kissed her then, no small feat considering she was still holding Calista, who struggled to be set free. "Wait, wait," Amy said, laughing. She set Calista on her feet, but kept hold of her hand. Then she lifted her face to be kissed again.

"I've been a fool," he said when they finally broke apart. "I realized it months ago, but I figured it might be best to give you time to finish your community service and to think about everything before I came here to beg you to forgive me."

"There's nothing for me to forgive. *I'm* the one who needs to be forgiven."

"You only did what you had to do. It took me a while to see that. What was *my* excuse for being so inflexible and hardheaded?"

Although Calista was tugging at Amy's hand in an effort to escape her grip, Amy leaned forward and kissed him again. "Stop. I don't care about that. You're here. That's all that matters."

Bending down, Bryce scooped Calista up into his arms. "Calista," he said, "do you want to go back to see Stella and Susan and live in my house again?"

"Stella! Susan!" she shouted. Her eyes danced with excitement.

"How about you?" Bryce said softly.

"Are you asking if I want to come back as a nanny to the girls?"

"I'm asking if you'll marry me and come back as Mrs. Bryce Hathaway."

Amy didn't have to think about her answer. "Yes!" she shouted just as loudly as Calista had only moments before. Then she threw her arms around him and her daughter and knew that if she lived to be one hundred, she would never again be as happy as she was today.

* * * * *

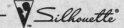

SPECIAL EDITION™

Coming in November to
Silhouette Special Edition
The fifth book in the exciting continuity

THE PARKS EMPIRE

DARK SECRETS. OLD LIES. NEW LOVES.

THE MARRIAGE ACT

(Silhouette Special Edition #1646)

by

Elissa Ambrose

Plain-Jane accountant Linda Mailer had never done anything shocking in her life—until she had a one-night stand with a sexy detective and found herself pregnant! *Then* she discovered that her anonymous Romeo was none other than Tyler Carlton, the man spearheading the investigation of her beleaguered boss, Walter Parks. Tyler wanted to give his child a real family, and convinced Linda to marry him. Their passion sparked in close quarters, but Linda was wary of Tyler's motives and afraid of losing her heart. Was he using her to get to Walter—or had they found the true love they'd both longed for?

Available at your favorite retail outlet.

If you enjoyed what you just read,
then we've got an offer you can't resist!

Take 2 bestselling love stories FREE!

Plus get a FREE surprise gift!

Clip this page and mail it to Silhouette Reader Service™

IN U.S.A.
3010 Walden Ave.
P.O. Box 1867
Buffalo, N.Y. 14240-1867

IN CANADA
P.O. Box 609
Fort Erie, Ontario
L2A 5X3

YES! Please send me 2 free Silhouette Special Edition® novels and my free surprise gift. After receiving them, if I don't wish to receive anymore, I can return the shipping statement marked cancel. If I don't cancel, I will receive 6 brand-new novels every month, before they're available in stores! In the U.S.A., bill me at the bargain price of $4.24 plus 25¢ shipping and handling per book and applicable sales tax, if any*. In Canada, bill me at the bargain price of $4.99 plus 25¢ shipping and handling per book and applicable taxes**. That's the complete price and a savings of at least 10% off the cover prices—what a great deal! I understand that accepting the 2 free books and gift places me under no obligation ever to buy any books. I can always return a shipment and cancel at any time. Even if I never buy another book from Silhouette, the 2 free books and gift are mine to keep forever.

235 SDN DZ9D
335 SDN DZ9E

Name	(PLEASE PRINT)	
Address	Apt.#	
City	State/Prov.	Zip/Postal Code

Not valid to current Silhouette Special Edition® subscribers.

Want to try two free books from another series?
Call 1-800-873-8635 or visit www.morefreebooks.com.

* Terms and prices subject to change without notice. Sales tax applicable in N.Y.
** Canadian residents will be charged applicable provincial taxes and GST.
All orders subject to approval. Offer limited to one per household.
® are registered trademarks owned and used by the trademark owner and or its licensee.

SPED04R

©2004 Harlequin Enterprises Limited

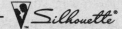

SPECIAL EDITION™

presents

an emotional debut

THE WAY TO A WOMAN'S HEART

(SSE #1650, available November 2004)

by

Carol Voss

It had been two years since her husband's death in the line of duty, and Nan Kramer was still struggling to raise her children in peace. But when her son flirted with crime to impress his friends, family friend and local cop David Elliott came to the rescue. David had always believed that cops and families didn't mix, but he couldn't ignore the sparks of attraction that ignited whenever he was around Nan—and neither could she. Could they overcome the odds and find happiness together?

Don't miss this beautiful story—only from Silhouette Books!

Available at your favorite retail outlet.

SPECIAL EDITION™

presents

bestselling author

Susan Mallery's

next installment of

Watch how passions flare under the hot desert sun for these rogue sheiks!

DESERT ROGUES

THE SHEIK & THE PRINCESS BRIDE

(SSE #1647, available November 2004)

Flight instructor Billie Van Horn's sexy good looks and charming personality blew Prince Jefri away from the moment he met her. Their mutual love burned hot, but when the Prince was suddenly presented with an arranged marriage, Jefri found himself unable to love the woman he had or have the woman he loved. Could Jefri successfully trade tradition for true love?

Available at your favorite retail outlet.

COMING NEXT MONTH